TIPPED IN FROST AND BLOOD

LUNA LAURIER

Tipped in Frost and Blood
Book 1.5 of the Shadow and Moonlight Series

Story and Art Copyright © 2023 Luna Laurier
Cover Design by Luna Laurier
Editing by Natalie Cammaratta & The Fiction Fix
Illustrations by Huangja

IDENTIFIERS
ASIN B0CNNQCVJ5 (eBook) | ISBN 978-1-962409-04-9
(Paperback) | ISBN 979-8-870334-56-1 (Amazon Paperback) |
ISBN 978-1-962409-05-6 (Hardcover)

For business inquiries email lunalaurierbooks@gmail.com

First Edition: December 2023

CONTENT WARNING

While these are not all the focus, please be aware that this series
contains scenes of the following

Alcohol,
Anxiety
Assault
Blood
Chronic Illness
Death
Depression
Death Of A Child
Discussion Of Child Loss
Death In Childbirth
Emotional Violence
Fire
Hospitalization
Kidnapping
Loss of a Spouse
Murder
Medical Content
Mention Of Self-Harm

Mention of Rape
Misogyny
Needles
Physical Violence
Panic Attacks
Profanity
Pregnancy
Poisoning
PTSD
Reincarnation
Sexual Assault
Sexually Explicit Scenes
Smoking
Suicidal Ideation (Implied)
Terminal Illness
Torture
Violence
War

For the most up to date list visit lunalaurier.com

To those in dark places.
You are not alone.
You will find your way out.
One step at a time.

PROLOGUE

DAMIEN

December 21st, 2012 - One year ago

The house smelled of roasted meat and spiced apples, full of laughter and conversation—the Solstice celebration well underway. My eyes drifted over the various items decorating Vincent and Anna's home— the candles, the garland, the massive tree adorned with all sorts of ornaments.

When had I last put up a tree?

For a long while after Lucia passed, I'd continued the tradition, searching for trees just as I had every year with her, decorating them with the ornaments that had survived the decades. As the years went on, and she hadn't returned...

Twenty years went by. Then thirty. Then fifty, and slowly, the magic—the joy—died out. I stopped searching the forest to pick the perfect tree, stopped unpacking the ornaments we'd collected and made over the centuries.

Then, I stopped decorating all together.

At some point, a tree began appearing in the living room each year, and decorations adorned the house. Barrett and Ethel had taken it upon themselves to decorate. I didn't stop them.

I still participated in the festivities, still humored my brothers and their need to celebrate, and a part of me tried to find happiness in their joy.

"Barrett, don't you dare touch that turkey!" Anna's chastising voice caught my attention, and I looked up just as Barrett retracted his hand where she had smacked him.

"What? I just want a taste!" he whined.

What was I even doing here anymore? What was the point in all this?

Vincent leaned in to press a kiss to Anna's forehead, and Ethel emerged from the kitchen with a platter full of roasted vegetables Anna had spent the past few months growing. Zephyr, Cole, James, and Thalia followed close behind her with platters of more side dishes.

I couldn't do this anymore, couldn't stand to face another Solstice without her.

I wouldn't.

CHAPTER 1

CASSIE

They say fall represents change, a time when nature and her children embrace the seasonal rest to reawaken with renewed life in the spring. Fall brought that very change in my life. My entire world.

Nearly two months ago, I'd been a normal human, attending college, trying to hold onto a secret, but it was one I no longer wanted to keep. It had been easier to hide when it was one friend, but now that I had so many people I cared for, it threatened to pull me under.

Now? Now, the world was far larger, filled with monsters lingering in the shadows and gods tugging invisible strings to plunge us into chaos whenever they chose.

Now, I was a demi-goddess trapped in a mortal form that couldn't sustain my powers—the powers that should be the key to our salvation would put me in an early grave.

Now, I had a mate. One who'd been searching for me for over a century when all others had given up hope. One who'd saved me when I didn't know I needed saving, given me hope that I might get to enjoy what time I have left in this life, and for the first time, I had a purpose, a reason to continue forward.

Fall was the season of change, yes, but what would winter, with its bitter, icy bite, bring?

Unease settled in the pit of my stomach as I stood on our front porch, staring out onto the dimly lit street. Guilt and dread clung to my very soul after what I'd done, beckoning me into the depths of a bottomless chasm—one I'd stared down into for the last two weeks.

My eyes fell to my hands, delicate, fractured crystals descending into my palms as I rested my elbows on the front porch railing. The snowflakes transformed, no longer the pleasant sight of ice and frost. No, they'd turned to ashes... Marcus' ashes, every bit of life I'd burned away in a matter of seconds. Ashes collected and built, covering my skin until it was all I could see. I swallowed, blinking in hopes it might go away, but it never did.

There was no escaping the bruises, cuts, and burns marring my skin as a reminder of what I'd endured at his hands, no escaping the death that now marked *my* hands.

Thank you.

I drew a deep, shaky breath, chasing Marcus' final words from my mind before the bile—

My stomach turned, and I tried to focus on breathing, tried not to throw up, but it wasn't enough. I hurried down the stairs, hand cupped over my mouth as I held it back before doubling over the snow-dusted grass and heaving.

"Shit," I breathed. Nothing came up, but still my body heaved again and again. Finally, it settled and I shivered.

God, I was a mess, struggling to get any sleep I could. There were times when I'd lose myself in training with Damien and the others, in the distracting jokes and laughter they always tried to drum up, or in painting and reading. More often, though, I couldn't pull myself out of the pit; there were too many nights I'd find myself trapped in the nightmares unable to escape until Damien shook me awake.

He got what he deserved.

I ignored the voice in the back of my mind, the terrible one that remained hidden for the most part. I hadn't been able to escape it; it seemed to always be there, waiting, rising up whenever it pleased, just as it had the night I'd given into its wishes. Though I dreaded to acknowledge it, I couldn't deny the truth of the words she whispered to me, whoever she was. If she was a darker part of me Marcus had created, or perhaps a version of me from a past life, I didn't know. I didn't care to know.

It wasn't that I felt guilt for killing him. He deserved to be put down, *needed* to be, for the danger he posed to so many. The way I'd done it, though... I feared for the way I'd looked as I burned him alive.

Damien didn't speak of it, and I never asked—couldn't—for fear of just what he'd seen in my eyes that night, in my expression. Had I smiled? Had I laughed as his insides boiled and his skin blistered? I shoved the thought back as my stomach turned, the phantom sounds of the flame somehow trapped in my ears, the smell of burning flesh in my nose.

Both my parents and Kat had been blowing up my phone the last two weeks. I'd managed to placate Mom and Dad with excuses that I was bogged down with mid-terms, and the guilt constantly tore at me for lies that had spiraled out of control, the lies that led them to believe I was still attending classes. I knew they were worried, and I had a sneaking suspicion Kat knew something was wrong, but she didn't let on when we talked. Things had finally seemed to start improving between us on my birthday, but of course every bit of resurfacing peace had been shattered in Marcus' final act.

Even though he was gone he still somehow managed to ruin things, to manipulate and destroy every chance I had at peace.

While every bit of what had happened over the last month haunted me, another weight threatened to pull me under.

Why couldn't I bring myself to tell him about my condition? *Just tell him the truth.*

I hadn't suffered any attacks since I'd been held in that cell, since Marcus had used me as a tool to get back at Damien for the loss of his mate— a loss Damien had nothing to do with. Outside of suffering the recoil when I'd visited Damien's memories, and a few times where I could feel my heart pounding, I feared an attack might crash into me, nothing ever came. Had Cole's manipulation of my blood done something to me? Had gaining access to my magic and learning to wield it done something to slow the damage?

No, I wasn't that lucky.

Delicate snowflakes drifted through the air once more, their form no longer that of my nightmares. The subtle glow of the streetlights illuminated them as they fell to the ground, collecting in a soft blanket that managed to stick for the first time. They likely wouldn't last, though—they would melt away by the morning light, vanishing as if they'd never been there to begin with.

Would it be like I'd never been here to begin with when I eventually faded?

My gaze lifted to the street in front of the house... *our* house. I was still adjusting to that—adjusting to, well, *everything*. The weight of it all sometimes left me needing to step back. I'd compartmentalized most of it to cope, but how much longer could I carry it all before I fell?

I drew in a deep breath and turned to head back inside, the cold night air permeating my sweater. The old door creaked and groaned as I closed it behind me, the click of the doorknob a harsh contrast to the deafening silence. There was no soul but my own in this space, no warm arms to hold me.

Still, I always felt as if someone or something was watching me. Always watching.

Perhaps it was paranoia left from when Marcus *tethered* himself to me and forced his way into my dreams and mind. The bite of my nails dragged me back, and I realized I'd clenched my fists so tightly I'd nearly broken skin. I lifted my hand, eyeing the reddened, crescent indentions on my palm. My eyes drifted to the healing cuts and bruises on my arm, each mark a reminder of what Marcus had done to me in that cell. The scrapes were gone, and the bruising had faded from a deep purple to a softer yellow and light brown, but the cuts still remained, still stung with the phantom touch of his knife.

My eyes drifted to the clock on the wall, the tick, tick, tick reaching my ears as I passed it. It would likely be a couple more hours before Damien returned from his patrol. He hated leaving me here, but with how few warriors served The Order, and the fact that the darklings were now hunting in packs, they'd had to up the number of immortals on each patrol team. Three teams were divided up to scout the north, central, and south sectors of the city of Johnstown. They were stretched thinner than ever now, and Damien was needed out there more than he was needed here with me.

At least, that's what I kept telling myself to get through the night.

Despite that, the selfish desires held me in a chokehold, leaving me desperate for him to come back to me, to not risk his life. My skin crawled as my mind wandered, wondering if he might, in fact, be fighting for his life at that very moment. I shook my head, trying not to think about it.

He's going to be okay; stop stressing yourself out.

I made my way up the stairs, the groan of the wood with each step leaving my skin crawling at the thought that I might be alerting something to my location so it might hunt me down.

For a time, I'd been terrified of the darklings coming to find me in the house when I was alone. I constantly found myself looking over my shoulder on sleepless nights, ones where I'd roam the house to keep from waking Damien from the rest he needed. Damien had assured me numerous times that darklings never entered homes unless led there, that they stuck to the streets of the city where humans and immortals gathered—easy prey for the picking.

What if that changed? Their behavior had been different in the last couple of months. What if that changed too, and we weren't safe in our own home?

I shoved down the fear as I made it to the top of the stairs. Just as I turned to head toward our room, wood creaked on the first floor and I stiffened, my stomach plummeting. My voice was a near squeak as I called out, hopeful to hear Damien respond and not the shriek of a darkling. "D-Damien?"

"It's me, *mea luna*," Damien responded, his voice soft and reassuring.

I stumbled down the stairs, eager to see him, to make sure that he wasn't harmed. He sounded okay, albeit worried on my account. I couldn't help but smile at that, considering he'd been the one facing off against monsters that could tear him apart.

As the emerald foyer came into view, my heart swelled at the sight of him, his lips curving into a guilty smile as his eyes found me.

"Did I wake you?" he asked.

"No," I said as I rushed for him, but I stopped short of leaping into his arms, expecting him to be covered in blood. My eyes fell over his black leather armor and the sheathed throwing knives strapped to his chest.

"My team encountered no darklings tonight, so you can take a breath," he teased, and I wrapped my arms around his neck. He pulled me in tight against him and lifted me off my feet, spinning me around.

Even if it was only temporary, the darkness that had held onto me so tightly receded, recoiling from the light of his presence.

CHAPTER 2

CASSIE

"Shit!" Liam grunted as his back slammed into the dirt.

Thalia rose to her full height after flipping the warrior -in-training over her shoulder, her cornsilk braid flipping onto her back as she twisted around to face her other opponents. Sasha and Zach, another pair of trainees, paced around her as they gripped their training daggers, both watching Thalia as they prepared to make another move. My eyes fell to Liam's waster as it slid to a stop before me. The training daggers were made of wood, but while they weren't sharp, they'd still hurt if a blow landed.

"Better get a tighter grip on your weapon, Liam. You won't last long against a darkling empty-handed!" Zephyr chided as he assessed the groups sparring with each other.

Damien halted his advance on me, and I stiffened as I realized I'd gotten distracted.

"Sorry," I muttered between heavy breaths. Sweat rolled down my back despite the cold winter air, and I focused on pacing my breathing. My grip tightened on the hilt of my dagger as Damien stepped toward me, and I braced myself as I blocked his attack before diverting his blade away from me, slamming my shoulder into his chest.

He grunted, hand clutching his chest as he stumbled back, and a charmingly crooked, smug grin curved his lips. "Getting more physical now, are we?"

I sucked in a gulp of air and gave him a smile that was all teeth. "What? Is the Lord of Shadows afraid to get physical with a demi-goddess?"

He blinked at me, his brows rising at the bite in my words, but his look of surprise melted away into something heated. "I'll happily get as physical as my goddess desires."

I huffed a laugh and bit my lip before charging for him.

"Don't get too cocky now," he said as he caught my blade with his. We spun around each other, our wooden blades meeting briefly with each swing. My skin heated as he blocked and evaded me. My stamina was falling short where his seemed near limitless, despite his heavy breaths. Given how my heart pounded, I only had another minute before I'd need to tap out.

I ground my teeth together, determined to win this match as he'd won the last two. Going for his back, I spun around him, but he side-stepped out of my reach and stuck his foot out to trip me. I grunted as I hit the ground, and a groan escaped me as I pushed myself up, irritation burning in my vision as I noticed a few of the recruits glancing our way.

Seconds after my boots met the damp earth, I turned to launch myself at him once more, and he took an uneasy step back as he lifted his dagger, barely blocking my blow again. I smiled at him, and it seemed to catch him off guard as he frowned.

Perfect.

I shifted my weight away from him, and he stumbled forward. He grunted as I kicked my foot out, hooking his ankle, and pulled it out from under him, my body nearly faltering as well, before I caught myself. His grip loosened as he stumbled, and my free hand shot out, grabbing the guard of his dagger. I twisted, pulling it from his hold as I spun around until I faced him once more, both daggers secure in my grasp, the wooden blades halted against his bare throat.

His chest heaved, his hands rising in quiet surrender as I stared into his eyes. "You've been watching Thalia."

"She's pretty talented at fighting off numerous larger attackers," I said between panted breaths. "I figured I'd take notes."

His lips tipped up in a smile as he took a step back. "Excellent. Keep doing what you're doing."

I handed him his dagger before throwing my hands over my head as I drew deep, even breaths, calming my heart. Just a bit longer and I might've collapsed. It was reckless, but we didn't have time for me to hold back, to tiptoe around my limits. I turned, my eyes passing over the training yard of The Outpost. Our onlookers seemed to have returned their attention to their own tasks, the numerous warriors-in-training sparring with each other.

Barrett was nearby, working with another flame Stoicheion user to train a recruit with the same fire magic. Flames sputtered into existence briefly before dying out when they couldn't maintain it. I'd seen the man training at Barrett's side a few times before. His name was Aiden, and if there was one thing I'd learned about those who wielded fire magic, it was that they all seemed to be hotheads, although some more than others.

He was short-tempered, insufferably impatient, and Barrett seemed to be the only one who could stand to be around him. It wasn't clear whether they were truly friends or just tolerated each other.

"Here," Damien said, handing me a bottle of water, and I thanked him before downing it. "Your skill with a dagger is coming along nicely. I've taught you everything I can about your Nous ability—all that's left is to practice what you know and push your limits. You can even try talking to me through thoughts alone from time to time, start working to expand your reach."

"I think I can manage that." I wondered just how far of a distance I could reach him from.

"Zephyr and I were discussing your Thiríon magic."

I blinked, my brows rising. "Thiríon?"

He nodded. "Do you remember how he can shift into a raven? That's Thiríon magic."

My heart picked up pace, excitement swelling in my chest. He'd been reluctant to add to my training over the past few weeks, had been furious with Selene's orders to continue it despite everything that had happened. "I can finally start learning new magic?"

He gave me a nervous smile, and for a moment I saw the hesitation that always came with intensifying my training. "I feel it's safe enough to try now. Zephyr!"

I turned in time to see Zephyr perk up from his own group of trainees.

He hurried over to us. "Your training going all right?"

I nodded. "I think I'm figuring out Damien's pattern. Maybe I'll be able to get him on his ass again. Last time was a fluke."

"Was it?" Damien asked, and the heated look in his eyes brought me back to the moment he'd taken me on that mat. My blood heated, and I tried to pull myself from it as it brought forth the need we'd both struggled to resist over the last few weeks.

"You better make sure Barrett's around to see it," Zephyr whispered, and I snickered.

Damien shook his head. "We were just discussing her training with you."

Zephyr's brows rose and his pale green eyes swept back to me briefly. "You sure you're ready for that?"

I nodded, touched that he cared enough to ask.

"Okay, uh…" He ran his hand through his hair, and I frowned at how nervous he seemed. "We can start in a few days, work it around your morning training. We'll start with an hour a day and work up from there, so we don't push you too hard and burn you out. Don't want another recoil."

"It happened one time," I groaned.

"One time too many," Damien added, and I rolled my eyes.

"Perfect," Zephyr said, his eyes lighting up. "I've got to get back to my group. Oh, Damien." Damien arched a brow, and Zephyr continued. "James wants us to meet at The Complex after training to discuss Cole's escape. He's got some stuff to go over."

"Hopefully he was able to recover something," Damien said, his eyes sharpening as his thoughts shifted to the traitor who'd slipped from our grasp.

I frowned. "Has James had any luck recovering footage from the cameras?"

Damien shrugged. "The SD cards were nearly fried when he pulled them out of the cameras. He's been working to recover the data, but it isn't looking good. Hopefully, we can get some answers as to how the hell Cole got free."

"I'll see you there, then," Zephyr said as he hurried back to his group of recruits.

My skin crawled at the thought of Cole out there somewhere, and I couldn't shake the feeling that he might reappear. After he'd escaped, I remembered the terrible sight that greeted us when we'd rushed to The Complex.

The shadows receded, revealing the familiar hallway of The Complex. Damien rushed toward the doorway ahead of us, Barrett, Vincent, and Zephyr hot on my heels. My heart lurched, and I came to a stop at the sight of a man slouched on the floor, his head hanging to the side. Thalia stepped out of the room, her face grave.

Damien knelt next to the man, his hand shooting out to check his pulse.

"He's gone," she said, and my hand cupped my mouth. "We've got two more dead inside."

Damien cursed and rose to his feet, stepping over the man's legs to enter the room. I followed, my heart in my throat as the scent of burnt flesh reached my nose. Two men lay on the floor, their skin charred in various places.

"What the fuck happened?" Damien breathed as he looked over their bodies.

"I'm not sure," Thalia said.

"Cole couldn't have caused these wounds," Zephyr added from where he knelt next to one of the fallen warriors.

I lingered in the doorway as Barrett and Vincent joined them inside. My gaze rose to the center of the room, to where the shackles hung empty—the only sign they'd ever been occupied Cole's dried blood on the floor, smeared toward the door, as if he'd been near dragged out.

"Did anyone see what happened?" Damien asked as he approached the vacant chains.

Thalia drew a deep breath. "No. James got an alert when the security feed was disconnected. When I got here to investigate, Cole was already long gone."

Damien's eyes lingered on the empty shackle in his hand, his anger burning a path across my skin, and he cursed under his breath. I stepped toward him, my pulse pounding in my ears as I avoided the empty stares of the fallen men.

"There's no way he could have used his magic to control his handlers; the shackles were warded the moment we learned he possessed Aíma abilities," Damien said. His eyes rose to the ceiling, and I followed his gaze to the security camera, the plastic melted, lens shattered.

A muscle feathered in Damien's jaw. "Zephyr, get every team on this immediately—Thiríon users in their beast forms and hunting his trail. I want him found, now."

The teams Damien had sent out that night followed Cole's trail until it went cold north of the city. My mind wandered to the possibilities of what he could be doing, what he could be planning. He and Marcus had been working with the darklings, that much I'd seen in his memories. Would he assume Marcus' role under Melantha? Would he come after me?

No, there was no doubt in my mind that he would. The pure hatred burning in his eyes when he'd looked at me in the cell spoke to the depths of his desire for not only my end, but Damien's as well as Selene's, the goddess whose war his parents had fallen prey to.

"Let's wrap it up for today," Damien said. "You didn't get much sleep last night, and I don't want you to push yourself too hard."

I wanted to argue, wanted to continue training, but I'd been more sluggish than usual today, and with the amount of training I'd undergone, my appetite had increased—the hunger was already starting to clench my stomach.

"I have patrol tonight," Damien started.

I stiffened. "I thought you were off tonight."

This would be his fifth night in a row, and while he always managed to catch a couple hours of rest curled up against me until the sun rose, the countless hours he'd worked over the past couple of weeks between patrols and the time spent overseeing my training and the training of others worried me. It was too much, even for him, and though he tried to hide it, there were times I'd caught glimpses of the exhaustion in his eyes.

"My team didn't encounter any darklings last night, but one of the other teams wasn't so lucky. Two were severely injured, so I'm stepping in."

"Who?" I asked, my heart lurching.

"Maria and Deacon," he explained. The names were familiar, but I couldn't place faces. "I don't know if you've met them yet. They're all right, but they won't be ready to return to the field for a day or two while they recover."

It was a relief that they were okay, but I hated that they'd been hurt to begin with.

I dreaded the thought of another night in an empty house and the entire afternoon alone with my own thoughts. "Do you think I could I go visit Anna while you're working?"

His brows rose, and his eyes softened as he took my hand. "You don't have to ask permission, Cas. If you want to visit Anna, go ahead. I can drop you off whenever you like."

"I'd like that. She invited me to visit and keep her company. It'd be nice to get out of the house."

He lifted his hand to brush his thumb along my cheek, and the feel of it left my heart fluttering. "If that's your wish, I'll see to it."

I melted into his touch, and he lowered to press a tender kiss to my lips.

Then my stomach growled.

He blinked, and laughter spilled from our lips. "I guess I'd better get you home and fed. Come on."

CHAPTER 3

DAMIEN

"It's been two weeks since he escaped," I said, irritation swelling in my chest. "Is there no way to retrieve the footage faster?"

James shook his head, settling his weight against the table full of photos. "Ah've got the card goin' through a recovery software again. Each pass takes half a day, and what Ah've recovered from the first twenty passes has nae been successful. Ah almost couldnae get it out of the camera."

I ran my hands over my face, and Barrett, Vincent, and Zephyr let out a collective sigh as they stood at my side, exchanging uneasy glances. That footage was the only thing that might point us in any direction—without it I didn't know what we were going to do. How had he gotten free? Was it one of our own who'd aided him? Was there another traitor in our midst? No one outside of The Order knew where he was being held, or that we had even captured him.

My hands balled into fists. Three warriors were dead when we were already stretched so thin, and the one person with any information on the darklings and their plans was gone without a trace. I cursed as I looked over the photos laid out across the table before us—the guards' bodies and the charred markings on the walls and doorway. Cole couldn't have made those markings. Even if the shackles weren't warded to prevent him from using his magic, blood magic wouldn't leave wounds like that, and none of the guards who'd worked that night possessed abilities that could.

So, who helped him?

Barrett stood in silence at the table, rubbing his fingers along his jaw as he stared at the photo in his hand. "Those weren't normal burns."

I glanced at him briefly. "I noticed that too."

Barrett slid a photo of one of the bodies to me. "This isn't something a Flame Stoicheion would be capable of. I've never seen burns like this before."

I had, but I didn't want to acknowledge the possibility of it being what I feared it might be. It would be several more weeks before we got the autopsy reports back, so our quickest answers laid in whatever footage might remain on that fried SD card.

"How good is that software?" I asked, looking at James across the table.

"It might be some time an' several more passes before we are able tae salvage anythin'. Ah managed to salvage a single still from the video feed, but it was before anythin' happened," he said, handing me a photo.

My eyes fell to the photograph; a fuzzy, corrupted image of Cole slumped over, his wrists suspended in the chains. Fury burned in my chest as the image of Cassie suspended in that very manner flashed across my thoughts—every possible way he and Marcus might have left those markings on Cassie's body haunted my every waking thought. I knew he helped, but to what extent? How many of her wounds were left by him? She had yet to open up about everything they did to her, but the bits and pieces I'd gotten were enough to send me into a rage.

"Whatever you have to do," I said as I tossed the picture on the table.

"How's Cas been?" Zephyr asked, glancing over at me. "Is she settling in okay?"

"I wish I could say she was better."

"Still having the nightmares?" Barrett asked, and I nodded.

"Of course, she's still having nightmares," Zephyr bit out. "She fucking burned him alive."

"Zephyr," I said, raising my hand to him.

"That's not what I... Shit," Barrett ran his hand through his blond hair as he fumbled his words. "I couldn't believe she actually did it but, gods, she was a fucking mess when you carried her out of that building. The way she locked herself up in her library for three days... It scared the shit out of me."

It had been a little over two weeks since Marcus and his men laid a trap for us, but I remembered it as if it were yesterday.

I feared what exactly had come over her as she stalked toward us that night, the molten veins stretching across every inch of her body beneath her skin. She hadn't been herself, trapped in some sort of trance. The moment she had come face to face with Marcus, when she'd forced him to stand as she pressed her hand to his chest... She almost seemed to relish in ending his life, her lips curving into a near smile as he burned, as he had cried out in agony. The look on her face when she broke free of it—the scent of her terror—still haunted me.

I hadn't wanted to continue her training, fearful of what the long-term repercussions of using that magic might be, the strain on not only her body, but her mind. Selene had been adamant about her training, though, regardless of the toll it would take on her body, and it infuriated me to no end that the life of her daughter—my mate—meant nothing to her.

"It's a miracle she's alive right now," Barrett said, the look in his eyes making it clear it was difficult for him to admit. It was a reminder of the truth I didn't want to acknowledge.

"We should do something for her," Vincent said, rising from where he sat nearby. "Something to lift her spirits, make her feel more at home."

Zephyr's eyes lit up. "Winter Solstice is in a couple of weeks."

"Shit, is it already that close?" I breathed. I'd been so lost in the war efforts, in training Cas and hunting Cole, the celebration had snuck up on me. I hadn't even had a chance to talk to Cassie about it.

"She always loved Solstice," Barrett added, his eyes going distant, as if falling into a memory.

She had. It had always been her favorite celebration across all of her past lives. She always had a fondness for the falling snow, the games and festivities our people held to celebrate the end of the season.

"I think that's a great idea," I said, a smile curving my lips as I thought of how she might light up when we shared our traditions. Would she remember any of them?

"We'll go all out," Barrett said. "Make it the biggest one we've had in years."

It was my turn to host the celebrations, and with the chaos of everything, I'd fallen severely behind on preparations. Vincent and Anna had hosted the previous Winter Solstice celebration, and it was a blessing that they'd hosted then. There was no way she could handle the stress of planning and organizing while pregnant. It was enough that Vincent had been on high alert with her health and well-being in the months since they'd found out.

"Who's in charge of the gift exchange?" Vincent asked.

"I did it last year," Zephyr said.

"I call dibs on that," Barrett chimed in. I narrowed my eyes at him as a smug grin curved his lips, and he feigned a look of innocence. "What?"

"Don't make me regret this." I had a feeling I would.

He placed a hand to his chest, gasping as if he were insulted. "I would *never*."

CHAPTER 4
CASSIE

"Don't mind the mess," Anna said apologetically as she led me through her gardens growing along the mountain side. "It's a bit chaotic around here with the end of the season. I got most of it harvested, but there's still so much to do."

Stone retention walls formed numerous terraces along the slopes behind her house. The beds overflowed with various kinds of greenery, flowers painted the hillside in bright shades of pinks, purples, and reds, vines spilled over some of the walls, littered with what looked like pumpkins and other squash ready to be harvested. Before us, at the base of the slope, stood a glass greenhouse.

"Anna, stop. I'm here to help, not judge." I said. "I can only imagine how difficult it is to do all this while pregnant."

She gave me a sheepish grin as she opened the door and led me inside. I was stunned by how warm it was inside compared to the bite of the icy outside air.

"I'm just glad the morning sickness is mostly past," she said, reaching for a large pot, and I hurried over to her, taking it before she could get far.

"You're not supposed to be lifting heavy things. That's why I'm here," I chided, and she snickered before pointing me to where she wanted it.

"Was it bad?" I asked as I set it on top of the wooden table. My gaze fell over the grain of the wood before I slid my hand over the rough surface, something humming in response beneath my skin. My eyes lit up when I realized the table was alive, roots anchored into the soil at the base.

"The worst," she admitted. "The mint tea helped some. That night I came to sit with you while Damien and the others were on patrol was one of the few nights I wasn't glued to the toilet. I don't understand why they call it morning sickness. It pops up at all hours of the day and night."

I grimaced. "That's gotta be rough."

"It was. You should shed that coat," she said, nodding to my jacket. "You'll be sweating in here in no time. There's a coat hook by the door."

I slipped out of my jacket and hung it up before returning to her. My eyes passed over the lush greenery vining along the walls and ceilings from pots nestled in macrame nets. "It's so beautiful in here."

Her smile widened, her sepia-brown cheeks turning a faint shade of pink. "Thank you. Vincent had it built for me twenty years ago when I kept complaining about gardening in the snow with low tunnels."

"Low tunnels?" I asked.

"They're basically hoops that you run white fabric over to protect the plants from the frost. They work, but they can be a bit of a pain."

"Talkin' shit about me?" Vincent said, and we turned to find him leaning against the doorway, arms crossed over his chest. "And here I was coming to help."

Anna snickered as he approached, and he swept her up into a deep embrace. "Your meeting over already?"

Vincent nodded and pressed a tender kiss to her forehead before kneeling to press a kiss to her slightly swollen belly. My heart squeezed at the sight of it, of their happiness caressing my skin in warm, inviting waves.

"How did it go?" I asked tentatively.

"Not as well as we hoped," Vincent admitted, rising back to his feet. "James is still trying to recover the footage, and we've got no new leads on how Cole escaped."

Unease swelled in the pit of my stomach. Damien had been stressing over Cole's escape, and I hated how much time he'd dedicated to hunting him down the past couple of weeks—how little sleep he seemed to get.

"No point in worrying over it. He's not getting anywhere near you," Vincent assured me, and I smiled at the determination in his eyes.

"I'm not afraid of him," I said, and while I feared the words would feel like a lie, they didn't. I *wasn't* afraid of him. If anything, I'd grown eager to find him, to continue searching his memories. Whether it would be a pleasant experience for him or not, I'd yet to decide, though there was a part of me that didn't want to hold back, that didn't care if it hurt him.

His pain would taste delicious.

"What all is on the list to harvest today?" Vincent asked, and I blinked, drawn away from the venomous voice.

Anna's dark brows rose. "You're helping us? Aren't you on patrol tonight?"

"I've got a few hours before my shift. I don't want you pushing yourself too hard."

"I'm perfectly capable of gardening," she huffed. "Dr. Johnson said it's good for me to get some light exercise."

"And what did he say about how swollen your ankles got the other day?" he countered, cocking an eyebrow.

"My blood pressure was fine this morning," she said crossing her arms. "I was just on my feet a bit too long that day."

"Just take it slow, please," Vincent said, leaning his forehead against hers, and her shoulders slumped as she rolled her eyes.

"Yes, Daddy," she teased.

"Gods, I can't wait to hear her call me that."

"Her?" I said, perking up, my heart skipping a beat.

"Ignore him. We don't know what it is yet," Anna said, turning to head for a row full of countless fluffy greens. They almost resembled... parsley? But there was so much of it. Why would she grow so much parsley?

"I just know it's gonna be a girl," Vincent said, his eyes lit with something that had warmth filling my chest. Had Damien been like this when we were expecting Emilia? My chest swelled at the thought of it, and I wished I could remember, even a little. I wished I could experience that with him one day.

"Do you guys have names picked out yet?" I asked, kneeling on the other side of the row as Anna's eyes passed over the plants in quiet assessment.

Vincent beamed. "Sophia."

Anna huffed a laugh. "*If* it's a girl."

"It will be," he said with a knowing smile.

She elbowed him, and he huffed a laugh before she continued. "Vincent picked out her name a few weeks after we found out. We decided he would get to choose the name if it's a girl."

"Awe, that's such a cute idea," I said.

"And if it's a boy..." she started.

"Did you decide?" he asked, his blond brows rising as excitement lit his eyes.

Anna smiled, as if answering his question and she lowered her bare hands onto the soil, stretching her fingers out into the loamy earth as she closed her eyes.

"What did you decide?" Vincent asked eagerly when she left him hanging.

Her lashes lifted, but her eyes stayed on the plants before her. "Andreas."

Vincent's smile faded, and he blinked. "You..."

She turned her gaze to him, a soft smile curving her lips. "I thought it would be nice to name him after your father."

Something in the recesses of my mind saddened. I wasn't sure why, but it left me unsettled.

"I..." His silver eyes glistened as he blinked. "Really?"

She nodded with a smile.

"Vincent's father died during The Fall of Kingdoms," Anna said, and my heart squeezed at the adoration in his eyes. "I wished I'd gotten a chance to meet him. You and your mother always speak so highly of him. I thought it only fitting to honor his memory."

"It's perfect," Vincent said, wiping residual tears from his eyes before he pressed a kiss to her cheek. "We'll have to save it for the next, though, because it's definitely gonna be a girl."

Anna snickered, shaking her head before closing her eyes, her fingers sliding through soil as she fell into a strange concentration.

I leaned in to whisper to Vincent. "What's she doing?"

"Feeling if they're ready," he answered. "She's a Dendron user and can manipulate plants."

Plant magic? My eyes lifted to the abundant plant life surrounding us.

"They're ready," Anna breathed, her shoulders sagging, her breaths picking up a bit as if she were winded, and for a moment, it almost looked as if that bit of magic had taken more from her than she anticipated.

"Are you sure you're okay to be using your magic?" Vincent asked, his blond brows furrowing as he leaned in to stabilize her.

"I'll lose my mind if I can't from time to time," Anna said as she reached for the base of a plant.

"So, what are you gonna do with all this parsley?" I asked, eyes sliding along the length of the row. It was easily ten feet long and filled to the brim.

Anna's laughter filled the greenhouse. "It's not parsley."

She bit her lip in concentration as she pulled the plant up, and my eyes widened at the sight of the purple carrot.

I blinked. "Why is it purple?"

"There's all sorts of colors in this mix. They're heirloom carrots. This variety is called a Cosmic Purple. Try pulling one up."

I reached out to one, and she continued feeding me instructions. "Just get a good grip on the base of the stem so it doesn't break off. If it's too deeply rooted, we can use the fork to loosen the soil."

Excitement swelled in my chest as I wrapped my fingers around the ferns and pulled. I squeaked, nearly falling back as it slid out of the soil easier than I expected and my eyes popped at the sight of the rich red carrot.

"Ah! An Atomic Red," Anna exclaimed, smiling as she set her carrot into a basket.

"How many did you plant?" I asked as I handed it to her.

"I planted a hundred and eighty seeds," she said as she and Vincent got to work, pulling carrots of all different colors from the soil. "We'll store a good amount of them in the root cellar, some will be used for the Solstice celebration, and we'll gift the excess to The Order to help feed displaced families."

"Solstice celebration?" I asked, and Vincent's eyes lit up.

"We don't celebrate Christmas, but we have a winter celebration of our own, celebrating the end of the harvest season and the rest of winter," Anna explained.

The idea intrigued me, and I loved that they grew food not only for themselves, but for others as well. "Well, I'm here to help as long as I can."

"Perfect," Anna said, reaching for another carrot. "Because I've also got broccoli, greens, and some winter squash ready for harvest."

I reached for another carrot top, excited to see just what color I would find this time.

"What are you doing for Christmas?" Kat asked on the other end of the line as I paced back and forth at the foot of the bed. Damien had been on patrol for the last few hours, and I'd tried to lose myself in conversation for the last half hour. Was this what my life was like now? Nearly every night trapped in a state of fear and worry for Damien's safety?

"I honestly have no idea," I said, caught between Christmas and the immortals' Winter Solstice celebration. How did they celebrate it? Was it the same day as Christmas or different? I wanted to get Damien something for Christmas, but did they exchange gifts like we did? Would that be strange? Would it be weird for a human to join in on an immortal holiday?

My stomach twisted, and I began to fear that my presence might somehow be improper or get in the way. "What are *you* planning?"

"I don't think my parents are passing back through until after the first of the year, but honestly, I haven't talked to them for months. So, as of right now, I might be spending it alone."

"Still not getting along with them?" I asked before taking a sip of my tea, the warmth filling my stomach in the most delicious way.

"Yep. Last time we talked, it just ended in another fight," Kat said with a sigh. "It's honestly been nice not having them around."

I winced at the thought that their relationship was so bad, she felt relief in their absence.

An uncomfortable energy had built between my parents and me after I'd moved in with Damien so suddenly. Was it naïve and foolish? Probably, but there was nowhere I felt safer, and just the thought of setting foot in my apartment was enough to bring on a panic attack.

They could burn it to the ground for all I cared.

Mom had always been the understanding one, attempting to give me the room to make my own decisions as an adult. She always remained calm and sweet when we spoke. Dad, on the other hand, was frustrated with me, to say the least. He'd tried to be amicable after I'd moved in with Damien, but it hadn't lasted. I'd already gotten into it with him just a few days ago, when he'd tried to talk me into moving back in with them—panicked over the three days I'd avoided them after I'd killed Marcus.

How was I going to smooth things out? How could I assure them I was better off here, with Damien? Not only was I safer, but they were as well. They wouldn't understand. There was no way to tell them, not when they couldn't know the truth.

Melantha, the darkling queen, wanted me. For what, we didn't know, and if I lived with my parents, they might get caught in the middle of this war. I couldn't bear the thought of losing them, of them suffering the fate so many had.

"I'm so sorry they're like that."

"Eh. I don't let it ruin my sleep, and you shouldn't either."

Maybe we could invite her to spend Christmas with us, so she wasn't alone. I frowned then—Damien and the others didn't celebrate Christmas. Maybe I'd go spend it with her? Or maybe she would plan something with Cody?

"How're things with Cody?" I asked.

"Really good. He's gonna be traveling in a few weeks to visit family for Christmas."

"Maybe we could do something together," I said without thinking as I eased onto the bed.

"I'm sure you've got enough on your plate with moving in with Damien and stuff. I don't want to intrude."

"You're not intruding. We haven't been able to hang out much lately. I'd love to see you."

She hesitated, but said, "If you're sure."

"I'll talk to Damien and see what he's got planned. I'm sure it won't be an issue."

"Thanks, Cas," she said, and the relief tone in her voice twisted my heart. Had she really intended to spend Christmas alone?

"You're always welcome here," I said, and my chest swelled as an idea sparked to life. "We should hang out soon, maybe go Christmas shopping. I need to find a gift for Damien."

"I love that idea!" she exclaimed. "I'll be finished with midterms next week, and then I can breathe."

"Let's plan something as soon as you're finished with them, then."

"Deal," she said, a yawn coming through the line. "Well, I've gotta go. Got class in the morning. First midterm is tomorrow, and I'm dreading it."

My smile fell, and my shoulders sagged. Our conversations had felt short as of late. We used to talk until long after midnight, but now, we barely made it an hour before she would dip out. I should be happy she was even talking to me at all. There had been a time after Marcus had taken me that she'd grown so distant, I feared I might have lost her.

"Okay, good luck," I managed to say.

"Thanks. I'm gonna need it."

"You'll do great."

"We'll see," she sighed. "Love you."

"Love you."

The line went dead, and I lowered my phone to look at the screen. Only half past eleven. I let out a sigh and tossed the phone to the side, setting my tea on the nightstand before rising from the bed to head to the bathroom.

Damien and Ethel had cleared out half the vanity drawers to make room for my things. I didn't have much—just some hair products, makeup, and my medicine, which was tucked away in the back.

I reached into the back of the drawer, fishing out the orange bottles. Shortly after moving in with Damien, I'd managed to contact my doctor to refill my prescription. He'd decided to switch it up, trying out a different medication. They didn't see any need to bring me in for a checkup, as my annual was scheduled for next month. I dreaded all the tests.

More so, I dreaded telling Damien the truth.

I downed the pills and stashed the bottles back in their hiding place before trudging out of the bathroom.

How would he react? Would he be furious with me? Would he stop my training as he had when I'd killed Marcus? Would he try to cage me as my parents had tried for so many years under the guise of protecting me from something they couldn't fight?

Just fucking tell him.

It needed to happen. It had gone on for far too long. Damien had been going out on patrols nearly every night, and I wasn't sure when his next night off would be. Would it throw him off if he went out to hunt darklings with that knowledge? Would he get hurt?

I drew a deep breath, frustration building in my chest. This was so stupid, so unfair, to him and to me. We deserved so much more after everything we'd been through—the moments I remembered, and the ones still out of my reach.

My eyes drifted to the glass display case, the lights illuminating the swords and daggers on display. Moira's sword shined on the top shelf where it had always sat. I was eager for more memories to resurface, to know more of what my lives had been like. They were the stories I longed to lose myself in, more than those in my books. For while I knew there were darker, more terrible times, there was also happiness.

Turning, I headed for our bed, reaching for the book sitting on my nightstand, eager to drown out my racing thoughts. It was a new story I'd stumbled upon when I'd gone exploring the local bookstore, and I'd been thoroughly enjoying it. It was a story about a princess of wyverns who fell in love with a human, and that love became the death of her mother, the Queen, and the downfall of her kingdom. Perhaps it would be enough to distract me until Damien got home.

I climbed into bed and propped myself up on my stomach before opening the book.

For just a little while, I lost myself in the pages.

CHAPTER 5

DAMIEN

The wood floor creaked as I stepped out of the shadows and into the foyer. At nearly three in the morning, Cassie was likely asleep. At least, I hoped she had managed to find rest. I hated how little she'd gotten in the recent weeks. Some nights I emerged from the void to hear the thunder of her footsteps as she hurried to greet me. I couldn't deny it was the welcome I'd wanted for decades.

A hollowness crept into my chest at the silence that greeted me instead. I shouldn't be disappointed to not hear her voice calling from somewhere in the house.

She was human. She needed rest far more than our kind did.

Worry for my safety during patrols kept her up most nights since she had moved in a few weeks ago, and when she did find rest, the nightmares tormented what little sleep she got. I preferred the nights when she was so exhausted from training, sleep claimed her in such a tight grip that she couldn't remember her dreams when she awoke, feeling rested.

Sadly, those nights were few and far between.

I knew she suffered more than she let on, tried to hide the brunt of it. The sight of her awaking in a panic each time—the look of horror on her face before she realized where she was—it was all too familiar to how Lucia looked when she awoke from her nightmares of what she'd endured before I found her again. My hands tightened into fists at the memory of it. I hated that I'd been as helpless then as I was now.

Cassie tried to hide it, drowning it out with training and learning how to wield her magic, but I knew the memories haunted her. I hated it. I hoped the celebrations we had in store for her might lift her spirits, help her feel more at home here.

I carefully trekked up the stairs, eager for a hot shower to get the oily feeling of darkling blood and sweat from tonight's hunt off me. The buckles clinked as I began undoing the harness securing my throwing knives to my chest, and I carefully nudged our bedroom door open.

My heart swelled as I found her laid out on the blankets on her stomach, face resting atop her folded arm, her book laid open in front of her. A mix of our scents filled the room, and my heart skipped a beat at the rightness of it. The blend of jasmine and cedarwood settled a resounding calm over my body.

With each year that passed after her death, every piece of her had started to vanish one by one: how she smelled, how she felt against my skin.

It hit me hard when I forgot the sound of her voice.

I'd barely been able to keep my hands off her over the last few weeks, stealing her away every chance I got. In the mornings when I'd awake to her leg draped over my thigh, her head tucked against the crook of my neck, we'd end up tangled up in each other. During our training sessions, when we found ourselves alone, I couldn't resist the sight of her body slick with sweat as she sparred with me, the fire in her eyes when she became bound and determined to knock me on my ass. The first time she managed to take me down, I took her on that mat, feeling her come undone as she rode my cock. I'd even pulled her aside after one of our meetings at The Complex, too impatient to wait until we got home to feel her skin against mine. The intense urge to mark her in any way I could had been too unbearable.

Fuck. The thoughts alone had the all-consuming need rising again.

I stopped at the edge of the bed, taking in the sweet sound of each gentle, even breath she took. My eyes fell on her open book, her finger resting delicately atop the dip in the pages where she'd held it open as she read. What story dragged her from the pit of fear and worry? Perhaps I could find more like it. I couldn't fight the curiosity and slid the book from under her hand, taking a peek at what she was reading.

There was no fighting the grin tugging at my lips as I scanned the beginning of a detailed scene between lovers on the pages. I knew she enjoyed romance, but this...

I slid the bookmark into place and closed the book before setting it atop the bed. My eyes fell closed as I drew a deep breath, her scent filling my lungs and—

My fangs throbbed, threatening to unsheathe, and my gaze snapped down to her as the faint sweet scent of her arousal coated my lungs. This didn't seem to have been the only scene with this level of detail she'd read tonight.

No. She needed rest. I'd fed from her just a few days ago, had kept her up just the night before, our need for each other too much to resist.

A soft sound escaped her lips in her sleep, and the sheets whispered as she turned onto her side and... Gods, the shirt she wore—*my* shirt—rose enough to share a glimpse of her lace underwear, the curve of her ass peeking from beneath the hem, the juncture between those creamy thighs—

My hands balled into fists as I pushed past every instinct driving me to take her as my cock punched against my zipper. I fought the urge to crawl over her, spread her legs, and wake her up in the best ways possible.

One night. I could go one night without feeling her body around mine. I turned, making a hasty retreat to the bathroom before I caved.

Steam filled the bathroom as I braced myself against the black tile, letting the shower wash away the blood, the ick, the sweat. My gaze fell to my cock, still hard for her, still throbbing and desperate to be inside her.

"Fuck," I sighed. The mating bond was nearly impossible to fight. It made a male an absolute slave to his female, craving her blood, her affection, her body, every ounce of her very being. For the past few weeks, the bond had resurfaced nearly as intensely as the first time I'd felt it. She seemed to feel it as well, her scent flooding the room at the mere sight of me at times.

My eyes slid closed as I imagined her wrapping my hand around the base of my cock, the damned thing throbbing as I imagined the feel of her hands on me, her mouth, the sound of her shallow breaths and moans each time I took her. Images of her danced across my thoughts, of every curve of her body, the swell of her breasts, the caress of her breath against my skin.

Gods, my imagination got the best of me, so much so that I could almost smell her. I planted a hand against the wall as I worked myself in slow strokes and frowned as her scent of jasmine and citrus cut through the steam of the shower, growing stronger still.

Soft hands slid around my waist, and my cock twitched in my grasp. Her delicate fingertips followed every dip and swell of muscle down my stomach, and I shuddered. I made to turn toward her, but she pressed against my back, her breasts soft against me and Gods, I wanted a taste of her creamy skin.

"*Mea luna,*" I breathed, a grin curving my lips. "It's unwise to sneak up on a warrior."

She didn't speak, one of her hands moving up my chest while the other glided south, lower and lower, until her fingertip brushed the tip of my cock.

"Maybe you're getting rusty, *m'lord*," she said, a teasing tone coating her tongue.

My skin tightened, and the hand supporting me against the tile balled into a fist. I spoke, but I could barely get the words out as her hot breath danced against my back, her hardened nipples brushing against my skin.

"Maybe you're getting too good," I breathed.

Her fingers trailed down my shaft until she laid her palm over mine. I released myself, eager for her to take my cock in her hands, in her mouth, between those sweet thighs. She wrapped her fingers around me, and dammit if I didn't smile at the sight of her fingers around my shaft—just barely out of reach of each other as she gripped me.

"Why didn't you wake me?" she whispered.

"I—" She slid her fingers down the length of me in one wet stroke, from tip to base and back again. "*Fuck.*"

I had to stop her. I wouldn't last long like this, and if I was going to finish anywhere, it would be deep inside her. She gasped as I grabbed her hand, stopping her torturous strokes, and I twisted around to face her.

My heart skipped a beat at the sight before me, at the water rolling down her neck, trailing over her breasts, down and down until my gaze landed between her thighs. My mouth watered as I imagined all the ways I wanted to taste her. She tensed, and she made to cover herself, but I grabbed her wrists, pulling her against me.

"Don't hide. I want to see you. All of you."

She smiled softly, her eyes flitting briefly away from me, as if she still feared what I thought of the markings, of the cuts on her skin. I'd kiss every inch of her body, worship every glorious detail of her just to show how beautiful she was. No matter what scars marked her, she was immaculate.

"Perfect," I breathed as I traced my fingers along her hip, and a smile returned to her lips. "Looked like you were enjoying quite a good book earlier." Her cheeks turned a bright shade of pink and her eyes fell shut as she shuddered with each brush of my fingertips. "Seems you stopped just before you got to a good part, too."

Her eyes popped back open as she realized I'd read where she left off. My thumb brushed under the curve of her breast, and she shivered, her breath hitching. I loved watching her buckle under my touch every time we were together, loved watching her shatter on my tongue, my cock.

And I'd love watching her come undone for me again tonight.

I wrapped my arm around her, sliding my hand up her back, along her neck, and ensnared my fingers in her hair, tilting her head back to meet my eyes as I guided her back against the wall. Her pulse thrummed as I brushed my lips against her throat, and her scent, the subtle fragrance of jasmine flooded my lungs, her citrus body wash trying so desperately to mask it. I pressed a kiss to her throat, my fangs lengthening, throbbing, dying for a taste of her

Her chest heaved as I slid my hand down the expanse of her stomach—devouring the sight of every reaction I elicited from her, every twitch, every whimper as I continued down to where I wanted to be, and... *Gods*, she was ready for me, so wet and hot, and my cock ached to be buried inside her.

She gasped, hips surging as I ran my finger through her slick heat, and I pinned her in place as I ran my tongue along the curve of her neck before nipping at her ear. Her pulse thrummed beneath the surface of her skin in a heavy thump. I didn't have to take much, just a sip. Her nails bit into my skin as she grabbed hold of my waist, and I moaned as the sting sent ripples of ecstasy across my skin, the bond rising to the surface as it begged to meet its counterpart. I pressed a kiss along that pulsing vein, and her head fell back as I dragged my fangs over her skin.

Her mouth fell open in a silent moan as I slid my finger over her clit. My control wavered with each movement, and I held her in place once more as her hips rocked against my palm.

A growl slipped from my throat as the void in my chest rippled, eager to escape, to touch her, *claim* her. "Easy, *mea luna*. I just want a taste."

She tilted her head, allowing me access, and I bit down, her blood hitting my tongue, rich and sweet and—

Gods.

She moaned, arching into me. "Damien."

Fuck. I needed to be inside her, needed to feel her on me.

Not yet.

I released her vein and kissed my way up her neck, letting her energy, her magic, coat my throat, our bond humming beneath my skin, my soul satisfied to feel its other half so close. Her knees shook, and I took hold of her hands, lifting them above her head until I anchored her to the wall. Those hazel eyes lifted to me, drunken and full of need. I could lose myself in them. Her chest heaved, the sight of her breasts enticing me to nip and tease and leave my mark.

"I think where you left off, the male had her pressed up against the wall while his hand slid between her thighs," I whispered, running my fingers between hers, until I found that throbbing heat I wanted to fuck so badly. "Oh, but he didn't stop there."

Her eyes fell closed as she panted, her breath growing more and more erratic with each delicious stroke.

"Do you know what happened next?" I asked, gaze locked on her as I licked my lips. She didn't respond. "Why don't you ask me? Or do you already know?"

I slid my fingers up her center once more and her head fell back as she gasped, her voice shaking. "What happened next?"

"He dipped one finger inside her." I did so, and she moaned. "Then another." I drew my finger out, and with the next gentle thrust, I slid two inside. She gasped my name, and my voice descended as need tore at my control. *"And another."*

"I don't think I can—" I slipped a third finger inside her, and she cried out, her back arching as her body tightened around me.

"Oh, but you can. Look how good you take it, *mea luna*," My gaze raked down her body, falling to my hand as she rocked against my fingers. "Just as good as you'll take my cock."

I licked my lips, my body nearly vibrating with the need.

"He didn't do *this*, however." I circled my thumb against that sensitive bundle of nerves, and she bucked against me.

"Damien!"

My lips curved into a wicked grin, my cock stirring with each moan that breached her lips, each sound of my name on her tongue as I thrust my fingers in and out. Once, twice, three times, and on the fourth, I curled my fingers deep. She cried out, her inner walls tightening around me as she shattered. I eased out of her, supporting her as her body quivered against me.

"Oh, I'm not done with you yet." I leaned down to whisper in her ear. "I'm going to show you what I can do that a fictional male cannot."

She bit her lip, and Gods, the sight of it nearly brought me to my knees.

Her head fell back against the tile as I hooked my hand under her thigh and lifted it to wrap around my hip. The head of my cock brushed against her entrance, the sensation nearly enough to break my control. So close, just one slight movement, and I'd be right where I fucking wanted to be.

I released her hands to cup her chin and tilted her head to me. Our eyes met, and I kissed her deeply. She parted for me immediately as I swept my tongue past her lips, and fuck, she tasted amazing.

Her hips rocked forward, brushing her swollen flesh against me. I moaned into her mouth and fell in sync with her, slipping my cock through her wetness, the heat all-consuming and—

"Gods, *mea luna*."

"I need you," she moaned. *"Please."*

All it took was an angle of my hips and I slid inside her with ease. We both cursed as I sank into her, her body tight around me in the wake of her orgasm.

I gasped for air. "Gods, you feel amazing."

She rolled her hips, and I lifted her before pulling her back down on me in one smooth thrust.

More. I needed more.

My strokes intensified, each thrust deeper, harder. Her hands fell onto my shoulders, her nails digging into my skin as I slammed into her.

Not enough. Not *fucking* enough.

I pulled out, tugging her away from the wall before spinning her around. She gasped as I grabbed her hips, my fingers digging into her flesh as I lowered her to her knees.

My eyes trailed down her spine, to her ass laid out before me. Locks of her wet chestnut hair stuck to her back in waves, and I pressed down on her shoulder, coaxing her chest to the tiled floor. She obeyed, lowering herself, and my cock twitched at the sight of her, her thighs parted, exposing every inch of what I wanted.

Mine.

My knees hit the tile as I lowered myself, dipping just low enough to run my tongue between her thighs, barely brushing against that sensitive bud. She gasped, body shifting forward as she bucked, but I grabbed her ass, holding her against me as I ran my tongue down her center. Her body tensed, her breathes getting shorter and shorter until—

I stopped before she could finish, leaving her panting on the floor, and I rose, grabbing her hands before placing them on the edge of the tub. "Hold on, *mea luna.*"

She did as I commanded, the muscles in her back contracting with each shuddering breath. I trailed my hand down her spine, and she shivered. I couldn't wait anymore, my cock still glistening with her arousal. A gasp burst from her lips as I grabbed hold of her hips and in one swift movement, I thrusted into her, seating myself so fucking deep, we both moaned.

Her head fell forward on the next thrust, and then her shoulders lowered on the next, sinking lower until her chest pressed into the tiled floor. I grabbed hold of her shoulder, pulling her back to meet my thrusts as I lost myself in her.

"Gods, you feel so fucking amazing," I growled.

"*Damien! I—*" She broke off, crying out as she tightened around me, and I joined her, shattering into a million pieces as I came, pumping into her until I was left spent and panting.

She settled against the tile, and I braced my hand on the edge of the tub as I regained control of my body, my chest heaving as I struggled to get oxygen into my system, each breath drawing in her sweet scent.

I slipped free and looped my arms around her, pulling her against me as I eased back against the wall. She hummed a sweet sound as she curled against me. Steam filled the bathroom now, the mirror over the vanity fogged over, the warm water raining down on us.

"Next time, wake me up," she said, ripples of her orgasm still echoing through her body with each shiver. I kissed the top of her head, the world right in every way as I held her.

"Oh, there are so many ways I'd love to wake you up, *mea luna.*"

She tilted her head to look up at me, a bratty grin tugging at her lips. "Well, you'd better start in the morning."

Fuck, the sight of those lips, that defiant look in her eyes had my cock hardening already. I smiled back just as wickedly.

"I intend to."

CHAPTER 6
CASSIE

"You're next, spitfire!" Barrett called from the top of the course carved into the mountain side.

I narrowed my eyes on him. "My name is Cas!"

"Sorry, spitfire? What was that?" he shouted, and I let out an exasperated sigh. As if he couldn't hear me. Insufferable bastard. I didn't give him the satisfaction of a response and turned to focus on what stood before me.

My gaze trailed over the different obstacles for probably the fifty-millionth time. This pass didn't change anything, didn't calm the roar of anxiety raging within me. It wasn't as if they were new. I'd watched the other recruits complete the course for the past couple of weeks, had been excited to take a shot at it once I'd gotten further into my own training. From what I'd heard, the course changed every season, so it was never the same, the patterns always adjusting to improve the recruits' training. Vincent had told me of one season where the recruits had to swim under water through a tunnel system before emerging on the other side. The thought of being in a tunnel underwater left me nauseated, and I was thankful it wasn't part of the course this time. Tight places terrified me for as long as I could remember, and the thought of being trapped somewhere left my skin crawling.

Sometimes, there were three sections—sometimes there were as many as seven or eight. This course had four: half of them on the flat expanse of forest, the other half carved above us into the mountainside, so high that I could faintly see Barrett and some recruits waiting for me and the others to join them through the bare branches of the trees. Nearly half the recruits had taken their turn. Many had reached the top, and many had failed—some walking away unscathed, some with a broken bone or two.

Now, it was my turn.

I swallowed, nerves snaking their way into my trembling fingers, and I balled my hands into fists to force them away. A yelp burst from my lips as Thalia nudged me forward.

"God," I breathed, placing a hand over my racing heart, but when I got a good look at her, I frowned at what almost appeared to be dark circles under her eyes. "You okay?"

"Yeah, just drank a bit too much last night. I'll be fine," she said, waving me off. "But that's not important. Focus on the course. You've got this. I saw how intently you studied everyone's attempts. You'll figure out a clear path."

I nodded. Yeah. Sure. This was easy enough. It was just an obstacle course. But as my eyes trailed over each obstacle, my nerves spun out of control, my heart racing.

An obstacle course designed for immortals, not humans.

Could I really do this?

"You'll be all right," Damien assured me, his voice a near whisper in my ear. "You're far stronger than you were when you started."

I forced air into my lungs and gave him a nervous smile before stepping forward.

The other recruits broke into a chorus of cheers as I came to a stop before the first obstacle—something we'd done for each recruit as they worked their way through. It was amazing how much everyone supported each other. It had been a little overwhelming when I'd first been introduced to the recruits as Damien's mate. In the following weeks, I'd encountered a few who were less than savory, but for the most part they had all been very welcoming, despite the fact that I was human and not the immortal they had waited centuries for. None of them had ever outwardly acknowledged what I was, but I couldn't shake the feeling it had been a bit of a letdown when they had learned.

"Ready?" Barrett called from above, holding out a stopwatch.

Shit. Was I?

"Yes!" I shouted, giving myself no chance to hesitate further.

"Go!" he yelled, and I leapt into a run, diving into the maze of tightly packed, low trees. I hadn't been able to witness its creation firsthand, but I'd heard of how a Dendron user grew them in a matter of moments when the others started almost a month ago. The branches stretched out to form a loose net of limbs to avoid, and Damien's words flitted across my mind from his explanation of the obstacle course a few weeks prior. I ducked and dodged low hanging branches before leaping over others.

There will be times you may be forced to face many darklings; you will have to ensure you are able to avoid their claws. If you are ensnared, you are dead.

I gasped as a branch snagged on my braid mid-leap.

"That's a five second penalty!" Aiden called out from above where he stood at Barrett's side, watching with intense scrutiny. Irrational anger rose in my chest as I felt the weight of those judgmental eyes.

"Dammit," I breathed, pulling myself free before continuing through the trees, cursing when I ran into a tightly wound cluster that formed a dead-end, only to have to double back and continue down another path. With the way the trees were laid out, I hadn't been able to clearly see the recruits work their way through this portion, so there was no way to tell which path was the correct one.

"Ten second mark!" Barrett called.

My eyes shot to him, briefly meeting his steel gaze. *Shit.* Had ten seconds already passed? I hurried forward, ducking and leaping over branches that seemed to almost reach for me as I approached them. Half of those who'd gone before me had already completed this portion by the ten second mark, and the end still remained out of sight. I stumbled over roots and rocks jutting from the soggy ground before the trees parted ways, revealing the next obstacle.

"Fifteen seconds!" Barrett shouted.

My eyes shot to him as I slid to a stop at the edge of the first segment.

"Don't focus on the time! Focus on the obstacles!" Vincent called from behind me, though I couldn't see him through the trees. "Master the course first. Then, you can focus on your times!"

I turned my gaze back to what lay before me, across the barrage of more trees grown at odd angles to form countless hurdles and objects to maneuver around and over. Ropes hung from low branches, and I could faintly see some strung across the muddy earth where pits had been dug. I hadn't seen it from where we stood, but I'd been curious as to why those who went before me had been covered in mud. Some carried the wet earth on their boots and pants, while others had been covered head to toe in the stuff.

You're wasting time.

I shot forward, not letting the voice phase me, her venomous hiss seeming disappointed in the pace I'd set—already off to a far slower start than the others. The first hurdle was easy—a slanted wall—but each one I cleared became more and more difficult, my stamina depleting quicker than I anticipated, my heart racing.

A grunt burst from my throat as I launched myself over another, and I gasped as my shin met a hidden taut rope before I crashed into the muddy pit before me. A collection of groans echoed from the ledge high above where the others waited. I grimaced as I pushed myself up, spitting clumps of mud onto the ground as I braced myself on my hands and knees for a moment, panting.

Shit. This was ridiculous. What were the other recruits thinking seeing how poorly I was doing? What would they think of Damien for bringing me into this? I was supposed to be the reincarnation of their queen, the daughter of their goddess, yet here I was, covered in mud, far slower than any of them. Could I even complete this course?

They're watching.

The voice hissed in the darkest recesses of my mind, coiling around my thoughts.

They think you're weak. They think you're slow, that you're flawed. You're a failure. How can they find hope in something so broken?

My hands balled into fists in the mud, but I didn't listen to it, didn't allow it a chance to sink its fangs in. I didn't care; I couldn't let this beat me. I *refused* to let this beat me. I wiped the mud from my face as best I could and pushed myself up, trudging through the deep sludge until I climbed out of the pit and grabbed hold of the rope to swing across the next one, my arms burning under my weight.

My feet finally met solid ground again on the other end of the pits, and I found myself hopeful as I looked to the next segment. The air had grown colder with my training gear now wet, and I let out a shaky breath as shivers broke out over my skin.

"Thirty seconds!" Barrett called out. I hadn't even heard the twenty second mark nor the twenty fifth over the all-consuming venomous words that clouded my thoughts.

I wasn't even to the halfway mark, and it irritated me as my mind felt the need to remind me of two recruits who'd finished the entire course in that amount of time.

Weak.

"Shut up," I bit out in a harsh whisper as I shook my trembling hands of the residual mud and started for the narrow path that wound up the steep side of the mountain, leading to the third obstacle. My heart pounded painfully in my chest.

Halfway there. I could do this. I just needed to pace myself. Breathe.

My boots squelched with each soggy step as I reached the narrow path. Chest heaving, I inspected it. It was too tight to take head on, so I'd have to skirt my way along the stone face of the mountain. I hurried along the path, back pressed against the stone as I slid each step along the edge. At first, it wasn't bad, but as I grew higher and higher, the distance to the ground turned dizzying. I'd never thought I was fearful of heights, but sitting precariously at the edge of a ten-foot drop, a fifteen-foot drop, higher and higher... I stopped looking.

Foolish. Perhaps you will die and spare them the trouble.

I opened my mouth to respond, but a gasp replaced the words as a rock slid from beneath my boot, and I grasped for anything I could as I fell back against the wall.

"Cas?" Damien shouted.

43

"I'm fine!" I called back, unable to see where he was or what he was doing as my trembling fingers clung to the sharp edges of rock at my back, my eyes clamped shut. As soon as I could get my shaking body back under control, I continued up the path.

I let out a ragged exhale as I stumbled onto a wider, flat expanse of rock and soil. Time wasn't on my side, but I took a moment to slow my racing heart, ever aware of the possibility of pushing myself too far. Maybe I couldn't complete the course in record time, but I would complete it regardless. I had to.

"Forty seconds!" Barrett shouted from above, and I cursed, wanting to shove the damned stopwatch into his mouth to shut him up.

We could do it, make him eat his words. Make him bend. **Make him break.**

I didn't give the voice the satisfaction of a response, hoping if I didn't respond it might finally shut up and leave me alone. It wasn't as if he were doing it to pick on me. He'd done it for all the recruits, helping them keep track of their pacing. It was an annoying reminder of my shortcomings, though.

My eyes rose to the massive rock wall before me. I'd barely call it a rock wall. It was nothing like the ones I watched others climb growing up, lacking the colored stones to grasp onto. I had to either find edges and chips in the mountain face, or I'd fall, and there were no harnesses, nothing to keep me from falling ten to fifteen feet to the hard ground.

For an immortal to fall that far might only result in minor injuries. For me... I couldn't let myself think like that. There were magic users who might step in, might help lessen the impact for Damien's sake, but I didn't want to rely on that possibility as a crutch. I wouldn't be afforded that safety net in the real world if I ever hunted darklings at Damien's side.

No. I *would* get there. I *would* hunt at his side. I would make Marcus' followers regret turning against us. They'd regret ever laying a finger on me.

Icy wind skirted under my braid, chilling the sweat coating the back of my neck, the mud soaking into my clothes as I reached out for the first notch in the stone. I grunted as I pulled myself up before placing my boot on a cracked rock.

A blur of shouts and cheers reached my ears, but I couldn't seem to latch onto what they were saying, too focused on not falling. I gasped as the stone under my right hand shifted, nearly falling free of the cliffside.

Don't look down. The taunt in the voice left my insides boiling.

"Perhaps if I fall and die, I'll finally be rid of your annoying chatter," I muttered, grabbing hold of another and pulling myself higher.

I cursed as the places where I could grab hold of grew more and more sparse the higher I went. My arms burned as I held myself in place, searching for another rock. As I reached for one, my fingers grasped at air, the edge just out of my reach.

"Come on," I groaned, stretching farther. Just a little bit—

I sucked in air as my grip slipped, and my forehead smacked into the stone face before I fell back, the world flipping as my boots slipped from their perch. My heart plummeted as I did.

"Cassie!" Damien's voice rang out over the expanse of forest.

Wind swept in, hard and fast, the familiarity of it speaking to me in a quiet language that needed no words. Invisible hands grabbed for me, but it wasn't enough to stop the impact, and I cried out as I hit solid ground, air bursting from my lungs.

I gasped, desperate for air but none came, and for a moment, I couldn't move, couldn't turn my gaze from the sky above me, from the rock wall taunting me.

Icy air brushed over my skin, colder than the winter wind, and a familiar presence surrounded me.

"Cas?" Damien said, his voice full of fear as his hand rose to my face, his eyes latching onto something on my forehead.

I parted my lips to speak, but I couldn't breathe, my gasps coming up empty.

"You're okay. You're all right," he said, as if trying to reassure himself. "Slow breaths."

I nodded, but the moment I tried to move, I winced.

"Don't move," he said, his hand rising to my chest before he turned to shout over the ledge. "I need a medic!"

I tried to speak, but my words came out broken, air evading me. "...Fine," I managed on the little air I could pull into my lungs. "I'm—"

"You're delusional." He felt me over. "You're not fine. Stay still."

Another face appeared beside him, this one unfamiliar.

"Hey," he said, his presence warm and inviting. "We haven't met yet. My name's Luca."

I blinked up at him as he knelt at my side, a smile curving his lips. I'd seen too many of those confident smiles in the faces of nurses and doctors.

"Cas," I rasped in response.

"Can you move anything?" he asked, testing my right arm, feeling it for what I assumed he thought might be broken bones.

I lifted my arm from his grasp, flexing my sore fingers, and I realized faint traces of blood were smudged across my fingertips and palm from scrapes from the rocks.

"Good, that's good," he said. "What hurts?"

What *didn't* hurt? My muscles were sore, my fingers and palms stung, my knees ached, my head throbbed, and my lungs burned with each breath of winter air.

My heart pounded, each beat a painful reminder that I'd once again pushed myself too hard, and I cursed my limitations.

"My... head," I said, finally finding the ability to breathe again. "My head hurts. Everything else doesn't feel as bad."

"Yeah, it looks like you hit it pretty good," he said casually as his eyes rose to my forehead. "Sasha managed to slow your fall."

My brows furrowed. "How..."

"Wind magic," Damien answered before slipping a glance to the ground where she stood with the recruits. "Thank the Gods she did."

45

"I think you'll be fine. Let's get you down and we'll patch you up," Luca said, rising to his feet.

Damien reached out, as if to scoop me into his arms, but I lifted my hand. "Let me do it."

He hesitated, a pained expression flitting across his face, but he nodded, holding his hand out to me. He helped me to my unsteady feet, and I groaned, clutching onto him to regain my balance.

"Thank you," I breathed, holding onto him, thankful he didn't take control and carry me off in front of everyone.

Shadows converged under the roots and vines beside the rock wall, and Damien helped me toward the void. The darkness swallowed us, the familiar tugging sensation calling to something deep within me before we emerged on the ground near the recruits.

I almost wished he hadn't brought me here, where the other recruits could see my failure.

Sasha was the first to reach me, her eyes lighting up. "You got so far!"

I blinked at the look of joy on her face as she took my hand. Zach and Liam came up beside her, and others joined, their words of encouragement something I almost hadn't expected.

The voice was silent, slithering back into the furthest corner of my mind, as if it couldn't stand their enthusiasm and encouragement.

"Thank you for catching her," Damien said to Sasha.

Her cheeks turned a faint shade of pink, and she stumbled over her words. "My magic isn't quite strong enough to hold someone, but—"

"That was amazing," I said. "Thank you. If you hadn't, I might've hurt more than my forehead and then I'd be falling even further behind."

Her dark brows rose, and she shook her head. "Oh, it was no trouble at all! Please, it's the least I could do."

I chuckled at her obvious fluster.

"Back to your places. There's still more of you to complete the course," Damien said.

The group of recruits all moved to attention, their backs straightening as they answered in unison. "Understood!"

They left us, and as I slid a look to Damien I couldn't stop my teasing tone. "So authoritative."

He rolled his eyes, but a hint of that crooked smile I loved so much tugged at his lips. "Come on, let's get you taken care of before you get yourself into more trouble."

CHAPTER 7
DAMIEN

"How's Cas doing?" Zephyr asked hesitantly as we rounded a corner into a dark alley. The central sector near downtown was quiet in the late-night hours. "I heard she took a nasty fall from the rock wall."

"She's all right." I scanned the darkness for any sign of the potential darklings lurking, hidden out of sight. Two Lupai accompanied us, their shadowy forms rippling with each step as they paced at my side, blue eyes searching. "Thankfully, she didn't need any stitches, but she had quite a knot on her forehead. She'll likely have some bruising. It could've been worse, though. Thank The Fates Sasha stepped in when she did."

"You gonna have her step back from the course?" Barrett asked.

"Part of me wants her to take a few days to recover, but I know the time alone with her thoughts might do her more harm than good," I admitted. She was hardheaded, just as she always had been, far more determined than most, and there seemed to be times when the training helped her more than just physically.

I admired that about her, but I feared she pushed herself too hard in her attempts to reach the sun. Nonetheless, I would be there, at her side, ready to catch her when she fell. I would do everything in my power to help her overcome every obstacle standing in her way.

"The mud was a nice touch," Barrett said with a laugh as he glanced at Zephyr. "You should've seen her covered in it. I honestly thought she'd give up after she hit that trip wire and fell into the third pit."

One of the Lupai brushed against my leg affectionately, and I ran my hand over its head. "It'll take more than that for her to quit."

Zephyr turned his gaze to me, and I couldn't ignore the almost smug grin curving his lips. "I heard she turned your own dagger against you the other day."

Barrett whipped around to look back at us. "Fuck, are you serious?"

I huffed a laugh. "I didn't realize we were the topic of gossip. Clearly, the recruits aren't working hard enough if they have time to talk."

"I'll be sure to drill them extra hard so they aren't ogling you and your mate making eyes at one another," Barrett mused.

"That sounds like jealousy to me," Zephyr said with a teasing tone.

A cocky grin spread across Barrett's face. "You wouldn't be saying that if you saw the female I took back to my apartment a couple nights ago."

Zephyr gave him an assessing look, and I let out a heavy sigh, knowing I was about to be pulled into one of their pissing matches.

"You should've seen the male Thalia left with last night," Zephyr said, turning to look along the stretch of dark alley ahead of us.

It was faint, but Barrett's shoulders tensed, his step uneven for the briefest of moments, but instead of retorting he continued forward.

"Awfully handsome, too. What *was* his name?" Zephyr rubbed his jaw. "Shit, Damien do you remember what his name was? He's always at Stokers, with the viper tattoo on his throat? He's not part of The Order. Honestly, I don't really know the guy."

I rolled my eyes. "Don't you dare drag me into your lovers' quarrel."

Barrett's hand balled into a fist, and my brows furrowed, but Zephyr continued when Barrett didn't respond. "They were awfully friendly when they left."

"That's enough," I said, the scent of Barrett's anger burning the air like smoldering oak. "We're supposed to be hunting darklings."

I walked up beside him, placing my hand on his shoulder. "You good?"

He glanced at me from the corner of his eye and nodded. "Yeah. I will be."

Something had happened, and by the way Barrett responded to Zephyr's taunts, it was serious. Barrett didn't typically lash out like this. If anything, they would go back and forth with their own snide remarks, and Zephyr would be the first to cave to his anger.

Zephyr passed us, and I waited until he was far enough to whisper, "Is *she* all right?"

"She is," Barrett said through clenched teeth. "Let's just say the bastard won't be frequenting Stoker's any longer."

What the fuck had happened? "If there's anything I can—"

"She's fine," he said, his steel eyes sharp as he came to a stop. "Nothing happened in the end. No one knows what he tried to do. I don't even think *she* remembers what he tried to do, and I'd like to keep it that way."

I nodded, relieved that, despite whatever had occurred with this male, Thalia was all right, and the bastard would never harm another female.

He drew a deep breath, and that calm cool mask fell into place again before he lifted his eyes to Zephyr. "When are you gonna finally get your dick wet and stop being such a prick?"

"Gods," I breathed, running my hand over my face. *Here we go.*

Zephyr looked over his shoulder and opened his mouth to speak, but the Lupai at my sides bristled, cutting Zephyr off as they growled. Their icy blue eyes turned a blood-red, and their jaws split as they bared their teeth at the darkness around us. The temperature plummeted, the darklings' icy presence snaking over my skin. I grabbed my dagger, but I wasn't fast enough as two darklings launched at us from the rooftop.

A curse tore from my lips as one crashed into me, taking me to the ground. A Lupai snarled before it sank its teeth into the darkling's leg. The creature twisted around, hissing at my shadow wolf, and when the Lupai released its hold, the darkling launched at it, jaws widening to bite down. I smiled at the way it fell through the wolf, the Lupai's misty body rippling around the darkling before solidifying to attack again.

I found Barrett facing off against the other. Black mist swallowed Zephyr as he shifted into his massive black panther form before he launched himself at the darkling that had just attacked me.

A shriek pierced the air, and I pushed myself up as three more came at us from down the alley. Gods, five darklings. This was the second time this week a group this size had been encountered. I grasped my dagger firmly as they threw themselves at me, gangly arms reaching, claws stretched out to tear us apart. A Lupai intercepted them, jaws tearing into the throat of one while the remaining two came for me.

I sidestepped out of the reach of one and it crashed into the pavement before I sank my blade between the eyes of the other, bone crunching against the Elythian steel. It shrieked before dissolving into dust. Another slammed into my side, and I crashed into the brick wall, its claws tearing into my leather armor. The darkling flailed against my hold, desperate to get to me, jaws snapping as I sank my dagger into its chest.

It stilled, the fight slowly leaving its limbs, and I yanked my blade free. It crumbled to dust, and I slouched against the brick wall as I slid to the pavement.

Gods, I was so tired of fighting.

My eyes fell to the near frozen dagger in my hand, fragile snowflakes cascading around us. The icy crystals landed one after another atop the black and silver metal until the blade was tipped in frost and blood.

Eerie dread flooded my chest as the black blood soaked into the crystalized flakes, the pale innocence tainted by the darklings' presence. I feared that, despite how hard we'd fought, this world might one day fall to their darkness as well. We had barely defeated Melantha before. Would we fail to bring her down this time? Would this be the final stand of the immortals?

A tawny hand appeared before me, drawing me from my thoughts, and I lifted my gaze to Zephyr as I took it, and he helped me to my feet.

"Gods, they came out of nowhere." Barrett searched for any signs of others, but the silence stretched on, the icy chill that came with their presence vanishing. "And five of them?"

"The group that nearly took out Maria's team two nights ago was almost twice that," Zephyr said, crossing his arms over his chest.

At the mention of that night my mind revisited the moment we'd found them, the sight of Maria unconscious on the ground, gutted and bleeding out, Deacon clutching his shredded, broken arm as he and Owen stood their ground, protecting her until help could arrive. They'd been attacked by nine darklings, and their team of three was overwhelmed. Thankfully, none of them had been killed or bitten, but Maria and Deacon being out of commission put a strain on the teams.

"Have you talked to Cas about the Solstice celebration?" Barrett asked as Zephyr and I walked toward him to continue on our patrol.

The Lupai yipped and whined at her name, and I rolled my eyes. "She's not here."

They whined again before turning from me to walk ahead, and I couldn't help but feel as if they were pouting. The Lupai adored Cassie, and she spoiled them in return, always scratching their ears or rubbing their bellies. It was laughable, given their nature as some of the most vicious predators in the Godsrealm.

"I haven't yet, but I will," I said.

"Better do it quick. We've gotta draw names for the gift exchange."

Zephyr huffed a laugh. "Someone's excited."

"Fuck yeah, I'm excited. I'm hoping I get Cas," Barrett said, resting his hand on the hilt of his dagger.

I arched a brow his way. "Yeah? Why is that?"

"I think I'm gonna get her some lingerie," he said, wiggling his eyebrows. "What's your favorite color, Damien? Still black? Or blue, maybe?"

The void in my chest stirred, every instinct rising to the surface as if it were the first time I'd found my mate. I shook my head, forcing it back, but deep within me, the darkness pressed against the cage containing it, begging to make it clear that she was mine.

"You think she'd like that, Damien?" Barrett added, testing me.

Zephyr huffed a laugh. "You're really asking to get your ass handed to you."

"What?" Barrett's lips curved into a cocky grin. "I wonder if she'd blush when she opens it in front of everyone."

She would, and Barrett loved picking on her, eager for her to snap back at him. I knew why he did it. He wanted to see the hint of her old self, missed the friend he'd lost all those centuries ago. My hands balled into fists at my sides at the thought of him getting her something like that. Gods, the mating bond was making me stupid, territorial in a way I knew wasn't necessary, and yet...

I continued forward, because I knew if I responded, it would just feed into his game, but the need to claim, to mark and defend what was mine, was nearly too strong to ignore. Just the thought of it made me want to get home. I wanted to be inside her, to mark her in my scent so no one ever questioned whose mate she was.

Barrett rubbed his jaw in contemplation as he and Zephyr fell into step on either side of me. "Do you think she'd actually wear it?"

A growl crawled its way up my throat. "Only once before I rip it off her and take her."

Barrett whistled low. "Damn, and here I thought you weren't the possessive type."

"Barrett..." Zephyr warned from my other side as shadows twitched on the ground beneath us, the void pressing against the confines of my body.

"That's okay." Barrett nudged me with his elbow. "I'll at least get to enjoy the sight of her getting all flustered when she opens it on Solstice."

"You say that like you've already picked her name out of the pile," I said, looking at him sidelong.

Barrett shrugged. "You never know. Maybe I'll get your name and you can wear the lingerie instead."

Zephyr choked out a laugh.

"I didn't know you were into that sort of thing, Barrett."

He wiggled his brows. "I'm into a lot of things. Regardless, it would be priceless to see that ass of yours in a thong."

I let out an exasperated sigh, rolling my eyes as I stalked forward. "Keep dreaming, because that will never happen."

CHAPTER 8

CASSIE

Chains rattled in the darkness, the sound so brief, I almost wondered if I'd truly heard it. Shadows swam beneath my feet, dark claws brushing against my legs, the feeling familiar, as if they'd been with me for centuries. The rattling chains pierced the quiet again, and I lifted my gaze to the vast nothingness.

What was it?

There was a strange familiarity tugging at the back of my mind. Shadows wound and curled around my ankles, but I didn't feel fear. They weren't going to hurt me. I was their prisoner, but I was also their companion, just as they were mine.

Prisoner.

Chains rattled again, and I stiffened as something cold and hard wrapped around my wrists, tightening until the metal cut into my flesh. My heart quickened, a cold sweat breaking out over my skin.

My arms were yanked from my sides, the chains ringing in my ears, the sound too painful to bear. They grew tighter, pulling my arms so hard I thought they might be torn from my body. I gasped as the shadows receded, replaced with concrete walls.

Prisoner.

I pulled against the chains, terror sweeping over me, and for a moment my lungs failed to work. My chest heaved as I tried to breathe. I couldn't breathe, couldn't get free, couldn't... breathe. I couldn't breathe. My eyes widened. No. No, no, no, no, no.

Prisoner.

"This is where you belong, little songbird."

My gaze snapped up to find Marcus before me, his lips curved into the cruel grin that haunted me. His body erupted in flames, and I jerked back, crying out as he closed in on me. His hand shot out, fire coating his skin, and the scent of burning flesh filled my nose as he wrapped his fingers around my throat. The flames grew into a great pyre, eager to devour us. I screamed as it spread over my skin, burning me as the fire consumed every inch of my body.

Murderer.

CHAPTER 9

DAMIEN

A cry pierced the quiet air as I stepped out of the shadowy gate, and air halted in my lungs. I couldn't think straight as I rushed up the stairs, my feet pounding against the old wood with each step.

The door slammed against the wall as I burst into our room, the room that felt far too hot. "Cas?"

A soft moan pulled my gaze to our bed where she lay sleeping, her body quivering, hands fisting the sheets until her knuckles were white.

My heart launched into my throat at how her fear filled the air, pain etched into her face—the sound of her pounding heart beating so fast, I feared it might burst. Her chest was heaving, her breaths too shallow. *Fuck.* She was trapped in another nightmare.

She muttered something in her sleep as I hurried to her side. "Stop... Let me... Let me go."

"Cassie, wake up!" I shouted, grabbing hold of her to shake her, ignoring the fact that my gloved hands were stained with darkling blood from the night's hunt. She fought against my hold, nails biting into my forearms as she pushed away from me, but I held her tighter. "It's not real!"

Her eyes shot open, wild and full of terror as she gasped for air, and she looked over herself, feeling over her body desperately.

"It's okay," I whispered. Her eyes frantically darted around, searching for something... or someone. She always did. "It was a dream, *mea luna.*"

"Where..." she rasped as she twisted to search the room around us.

"We're in our room," I assured her. "You're safe. He no longer has you."

She turned her gaze back to me and tentatively reached out a shaking hand to touch my chest, as if she were afraid I wasn't real. I took hold of her hand, pressing it right over my racing heart, hoping she might feel it beneath the leathers of my armor, that it might prove to her I was real, that *this* was reality. Her eyes lowered, seeming to focus on the feel of it.

She didn't speak for a moment, and I couldn't take the silence any longer, needing to hear her voice, needing to see her hazel eyes unclouded by the terror drowning her. I lifted a hand to brush a stray tear from her cheek, and she flinched. The movement shattered me, despite the fact that she seemed to realize what she'd done and immediately relaxed into my touch.

"I think you should talk to someone about this."

She stiffened, her eyes rising to meet mine. "I..."

"It doesn't have to be me if you're not ready," I said, hating that she still didn't feel safe enough to confide in me, her mate. She needed help, though, and if she couldn't open up to me, maybe she could to another. "We have a therapist in The Order. If you're comfortable, I can arrange for you to meet her."

Her throat bobbed, and her eyes fell away from me.

No. Don't shut me out. Please. Let me help you.

"Do you trust her?" she asked, her voice uneven, and I hated the subtle tremble in her fingertips as she gripped my arm.

"With my life," I said, cupping her cheeks to lift her gaze back to me. Her hazel eyes finally met mine, bloodshot, and I brushed another stray tear from her cheek. "Salwa's amazing at what she does. She's helped many, both warrior and civilian alike. Even I've seen her in the past, when I couldn't handle it anymore," I admitted, hoping it might give her some confidence.

"You did?" she asked, seeming surprised.

Hope swelled in my chest as she seemed to contemplate it, and I continued. "I found myself in some very dark places over the centuries, and when there was nowhere else to go, nowhere else to turn, I turned to her."

I remained quiet, giving her a moment to sort through her emotions. Gods, they were so thick in the air, coating my lungs with each breath. Fear, anger, unease, sorrow—too many to identify.

"Maybe..." My heart soared at the first sign of her trusting me to guide her down the right path. "What if I can't handle it?"

"Then we'll keep trying until you feel comfortable. One step at a time."

CHAPTER 10

CASSIE

"Shifting is one of the oldest magics," Zephyr said as he led me through the woods at The Outpost. "It was the second house created by Selene before The Titanomachy, also known as The Titan War, nearly three thousand years ago."

I remembered hearing stories about The Titans, but to know such powerful beings truly existed was unnerving. It had been jarring enough to learn of the existence of the Gods I'd thought to be mere myth and legend only months ago.

It had been a couple of days since my nightmare, and thankfully, I hadn't had another. I'd spent the past couple of days losing myself in my training, pushing myself to the point where I couldn't stay awake at night and fell into such a deep sleep, no dreams could trouble me. How long would that work, though?

"My great-grandfather fought in the Titan War," he said, pale green eyes drifting to me briefly. "*Metavia* always spoke highly of him. Told me all sorts of stories growing up."

The name stirred something deep in my chest, and I frowned at the familiarity of it. It was the Elythian word for... Grandmother.

I lifted my eyes to him, and he offered me a somber smile.

"I never met him. He was the first of our family line created by Selene when The Twelve rose up against The Titans to claim their rule over Elythia." Though pride lit his eyes, there was sadness lingering just beneath the surface, and it brushed over my skin in cold waves. "He took a fatal blow defending Selene, but before he succumbed to his injury, he managed to land the killing strike against Hyperion, helping bring an end to the ten-year war."

"Your great-grandfather killed a Titan?" I asked, my brows rising.

His gaze shifted to me, and for a moment he looked saddened by my question, but he forced a smile. "He did, and our family has had favor with Selene ever since. We serve her with pride, each generation serving directly under the king."

"That's amazing," I said, a smile curving my lips as I imagined having such a proud heritage, to *know* the stories of the past leading up to your existence. The only one I knew held information on my past lives outside of Damien was Selene, and I was too shaken to speak with her after our first meeting. Memories of the past still evaded me, and I'd only managed to regain bits and pieces. It wasn't enough to feel whole, but just enough to leave me desperate for more, and I was *so* desperate.

"Shifting is very simple, controlled by your mind and will. Thought manifests into being," he explained, and I latched onto every word as they left his lips. "Each member of House Thiríon has the ability to shift into two different forms: one of the sky and one of the earth. Sadly, the ability to utilize both is based upon your own power and strength. While there are many of us who can shift into either of them, there are others who can only manifest one of the two in their entire lifetime."

"You can shift into a raven," I stated, remembering how I'd mistaken him for a wild one before I knew what they were—when he'd spied on Damien and me during our first date.

The corner of his lips ticked up into a smug smile. "A pretty one, I seem to recall."

"A nosey one," I corrected, narrowing my eyes on him as I crossed my arms.

He barked a laugh, and my eyes widened as black mist exploded around him, his body disappearing from view. The cloud of darkness receded, revealing a massive raven, his iridescent black feathers reflecting blues and greens as the light fell over him. All right, he wasn't pretty—he was beautiful, magnificent, and... huge. God, he was huge, nearly twice the size of a normal raven.

He tilted his head to look up at me, and I gasped as his beak parted. "While I can only take the form of a raven and a panther, you, as Moira's reincarnation can take the form of anything."

I blinked. Was this really happening? Was I having a conversation with a raven? I shook myself from the momentary stupor. "Anything?"

He nodded, and the shadows swallowed him whole again before a massive black panther prowled from their depths. I stumbled back at the sheer size of him, his shoulders reaching my waist as he stalked around me before nudging his head under my elbow in feline affection.

He took a seat before me, and my smile widened. God, their magic was amazing, and I couldn't wait to learn it all.

"You've shifted into all sorts of creatures in past lives, even disguised yourself as other immortals or beings when carrying out missions." His eyes narrowed, and his muzzle curved into a near smile as he tilted his head, his pale green eyes going distant for a moment. "I recall you using it in the most unconventional ways to get into trouble a time or two."

I frowned, curious as to what I could have done, but before I could ask he shook his head, as if dismissing the thought. "For now, I want you to choose an animal, any animal. The more familiarity you have with it the better."

"Any?"

"Let's start with a bird of some type," he said. "Mastering your sky form first will be useful to flee to safety."

I drew a deep breath, my mind running through the possibilities. "What about an owl?"

"That's a good start, but you need to narrow it down to a specific species of owl."

I'd drawn them in the past, had spent time sketching a live barn owl in art studies class last semester. The details remained clear in my mind, having spent so much time staring at the stunning creature.

"The more familiar you are with the animal's anatomy, the more successful the change will be. If you don't have a clear vision in your head it will fail," he said, shifting back into his immortal form before taking a seat on a nearby bolder.

"I just imagine it?" I asked hesitantly.

"Form the picture in your mind, imagine your body changing, your very being becoming that which resides in your thoughts. You aren't simply changing your appearance; you are becoming the creature. Wings instead of arms, talons instead of feet. Give into the beast's instincts. If you can't manage a successful shift today, it's all right. This is just our first session."

I drew a deep breath. It sounded simple enough. I just had to picture it in my mind.

It was, in fact, *not* that simple.

Zephyr and I had spent an hour training, but nothing had come of it. He chalked it up to exhaustion and decided to call it a day. It irritated me that I couldn't push through it. I wanted to change, wanted to know what it would be like to become something more than what I was. I wanted to fly.

"We'll adjust your schedule so your shifting training falls on the days you're not doing physical training," Damien said, taking my coat. "You've been going hard the past few weeks; it might be good to slow down a bit."

"I don't want to slow down," I admitted, pulling my boots off, and a yawn crawled up my throat. "It's helping me in a strange way."

His gaze swept to me as he hung my coat up, and something akin to sympathy dulled his amber and ashen eyes. "I understand."

Something fractured in my chest at that statement, because I knew he did. I knew how deeply he understood why the exertion helped me, even if the results were only temporary. Just as my medicine wouldn't fix my heart, the training was just another bandage. I would have to face them both eventually.

"Damien..." I started. He didn't have patrol tonight—maybe this was my chance to tell him. I'd put it off for far too long.

His brows rose. "What's up?"

My lips parted, my heart thrashing in my chest. "I, uh... I wanted to talk to you about something."

"Is everything all right? Did Aiden say something else to you after the obstacle course?" he asked, blinking as he drew closer to me. God, the closer he grew, the more my heart raged out of control, my palms turning clammy. What would he say when I told him? How would he react? Fuck. Where would I even start?

"No. It's nothing like that. I—" The doorbell rang, and I stiffened.

"That's probably Salwa. We got back a bit later than I anticipated," he said, and my heart lurched. I'd completely forgotten The Order's therapist.

TIPPED IN FROST AND BLOOD

"What was it you wanted to talk about?" he asked before he could answer the door.

Something twisted in my chest, constricting until I thought it might crack me in two. Just as the words formed on my tongue, I couldn't do it, not with Salwa about to be here. We didn't need an audience for this. "It's... nothing. We can talk about it later."

His brows furrowed, and for a moment, he seemed to hesitate. "Are you sure?"

I nodded. "Yeah, I've put off getting help long enough, and I don't want to make her wait in the cold."

He took my hand, the feel of his skin against mine soothing in more ways than I could explain. He leaned in to press a kiss to my forehead. "One step at a time. Even if it's only introductions today, do what you can."

I nodded, guilt twisting my gut.

"Salwa," Damien said in greeting as he opened the door.

"It's wonderful to see you again, Damien," she said.

A knot formed in my throat at her voice. Was I ready for this? What would we talk about? I'd never seen a therapist before. I couldn't deny how nervous I was to meet her, to speak to her, to talk about... everything. There was no hiding it, though. I needed help, and training wasn't erasing it, wasn't stopping the nightmares. I'd somehow managed to avoid their clutches, but they would return. It was only a matter of time.

"Cas, this is Salwa," Damien said, stepping aside to let her in.

She dipped her head to me, and a lock of her sable bangs slipped from behind her ear. "It's a pleasure to meet you, mate of my lord," she said, her voice soft.

My cheeks heated at the title. "Just, Cas. Please. It's... nice to meet you too."

She nudged her gold, round-framed glasses back into place on her nose, and her silver eyes nearly glowed against her dark brown skin. Her gaze swept back to Damien as he closed the door behind her, cutting off the cold air. "It's been a while since you've called me for a session. How are you fairing?"

"I'm doing well," he said, his eyes softening. "Better than I have in a while, if I'm being honest."

"That's wonderful," she said as she removed her coat. The genuine feel of her happiness rushed over me like wafts of warm sunlight in the summer. Her feelings were genuine, and something about that seemed to settle my nerves, even if only a little.

She turned her gaze to me. "I've heard a lot about you, Cas."

"Well, I guess who told you about me would determine whether it's good or bad," I said with a nervous laugh. "I'm sure if you talked to Aiden or some of the other recruits they'll tell you how clumsy I am."

Damien's eyes slid to me, his brows curving inward as his lips parted. Salwa spoke first, taking my hand, and something passed over my skin, something calming and inviting.

"All good," she assured me, the silver in her eyes so warm, it reached a deeper part of me. "I've been excited to meet you."

For a moment, as we held each other's gazes, the hesitation that had clouded my mind seemed to ebb away, bringing hope that she may not only give me the help I needed, but that I might find a friend in her. A smile crept across my face before I realized what was happening.

"I heard you came close to completing the course," she said as we headed for the living room. She was so cheerful, and I hadn't expected to share a casual conversation like this. I'd expected her to immediately begin dissecting my brain.

"Almost, but I couldn't clear the final stretch of the rock wall," I admitted.

"Gave me a fucking heart attack," Damien added, letting out a heavy sigh.

"I was so close. I just need to figure out that last bit," I said, almost eager to try again.

"You're just as bound and determined as you've always been," Salwa said, the smile never leaving her face.

I perked up at her statement and turned my gaze to her. "You knew me in a past life?"

She nodded, her silver eyes warm and endearing. "I did. In two of them."

"I'll go make some tea," Damien said before pressing a kiss to my forehead. "Let you ladies get to know each other."

Salwa's eyes lit up as she rubbed her hands together before extending them toward the fire crackling in the hearth. "Oh, tea would be lovely."

"Thank you," I added as I settled onto the couch, and he gave me a light nod before heading for the kitchen.

"I knew Elena and Lucia," she explained before I could ask.

"I've been eager for the memories to resurface," I said, pulling my feet up onto the couch to rest my chin atop my knees. My eyes drifted to the fire flickering in the hearth. "I can't explain it, but it's as if a piece of me comes back every time I remember something, as if I've been missing something all my life." I huffed a laugh. "That probably sounds cheesy."

"Not at all," she said, tilting her head to look at me.

My eyes shifted to hers, and though I wanted to believe she was just saying it to comfort me, there was nothing but genuine light in her eyes, her honesty flooding my mind with warmth.

She continued. "It's only natural for you to seek them out. Have you had many?"

"Not as many as I'd like."

"They will come. Just give them time," she assured me. "It's different with each reincarnation. Sometimes it's difficult, sometimes it comes more naturally. We'll work through it, and maybe I can help you navigate them."

Silence stretched on for a moment as I watched the fire work through the wood, my eyes feeling heavy.

"Have you ever spoken with a therapist before?" she asked.

"No. Honestly, I've always felt weird talking to people I don't know." While that was true, there was something about her that felt inviting, familiar. Perhaps it was because we had known each other in past lives, or perhaps she was just that skilled. Either way, the way she spoke to me didn't feel as if she were prying, but more like I was talking with a friend. "I'm trying to have an open mind."

"We'll take it slow. Damien told me a bit about what you've been through, and I'm so sorry for what happened. The Nous ability is a wonderful gift with such potential for good. I hate that it was used against you."

"Are you a Nous user?" I bit my lip, realizing that might have been a rude question. "If you don't mind me asking."

She smiled. "I am. It's one of the skills I use to aid those who are suffering. It helps me heal them. If you'd allow me, I can use it to help you, but not until you're ready."

Something deep within me recoiled at the thought of her entering my mind, hints of pain scratching at the edges. I stiffened at the feel of her hand resting against my arm, and I realized my breathing had grown shallow, my fingers digging into my arms.

"Sorry," I whispered, hating that I couldn't seem to get past the fear.

"Don't apologize," she said, her smile replaced with a look of concern. "We don't have to do anything you're not ready for. I won't use my ability until you feel safe enough. If you're not ready to talk about it, we can just get to know each other, and when you're comfortable enough, even if it takes a few weeks or even a month or two, we can cross that bridge then."

A smile curved my lips at her suggestion, and her words helped ease the fear a little. "I think that would be great."

It was as Damien had said: one step at a time.

CHAPTER II
CASSIE

There was a different energy surrounding The Outpost as I sat in quiet observation, resting from the morning's training. Recruits still sparred. Zephyr, Thalia, Barrett, and Damien still oversaw their matches, still corrected their stances and missteps. Despite that, I could feel an odd sense of excitement in the air, the warm and ticklish feeling falling over my skin like the sun's rays in the spring when the residual cold of winter lingers, wishing to stay a bit longer.

What had happened? What had I missed?

I shifted on the bench where I'd sat to take a break. It had been nearly a week since I'd fallen in my first attempt at the obstacle course, and I'd failed another attempt at the rock wall a few hours earlier. It had taken every bit of will power to try it again, the fresh fear of it leaving me shaking as I grabbed hold of the first rock. I'd at least managed to avoid the trip wire in the pits.

As my eyes drifted across the training yard, Zephyr briefly met my gaze, but he quickly averted his eyes, and I frowned at the awkward look on his face. Was he okay? Had something happened? Then as I saw Thalia and Barrett working with their own recruits, I realized someone was missing.

Vincent was nowhere to be seen. He hadn't been there during the course training earlier either. I figured he might have been tending to something else on the training grounds, but he wasn't here still.

My stomach dipped. Was Anna okay? Did something happen to her and the baby to keep him from training? No. I couldn't let myself think like that. Damien would have told me if anything had happened, and I knew if anything had, all of us would be wherever they were.

The sounds of The Outpost quieted as my eyes drifted to the trees surrounding us, blanketed in fresh snow. It was so peaceful, something about the forest beckoning me to wander. I nearly gave into it as something brushed at the edge of my mind, soft and warm, and I blinked, my brows furrowing as I thought I saw something move between the trees.

I stood, my feet moving of their own accord as I drifted toward the trees at the edge of the training yard.

Why is it taking so long for you to pick a tree?

I frowned at the sound of Damien's voice, but when I looked around, he wasn't standing beside me but clear across the training yard, seeing to the recruits.

It's just a tree. Pick one already.

This voice was different, annoyed, yet at the same time, it felt almost teasing. It was warm, like a summer breeze, and I couldn't help but find a strange comfort in it.

You know she can't just pick any tree.

I blinked, blurred images of two figures standing next to an evergreen tree that stretched toward the sky, full of rich green, needle covered branches.

The same voice filled my ears, teasing once more. *It has to be the* **perfect** *one.*

For the briefest of moments, one of the figures came into focus before I found myself surrounded by The Outpost once again, the memory receding into the depths. It was Damien I'd seen, but...

I paused. Who had stood with him? I reached back out, desperate for the memory to resurface, but it seemed to slip further from my grasp.

Something icy hit the back of my head, and I stumbled, yelping as I nearly fell forward. I rubbed the back of my head, finding bits of snow sticking to my hair as I twisted around to find Vincent surrounded by a group of children. The recruits halted their training, turning their gazes to them as well before the children pulled their hands from behind their backs to reveal snowballs.

"Attack!" Vincent shouted, and the children screamed and giggled as they ran for cover, pelting the recruits with snowballs.

I looked around frantically. What the hell was going on? Where had they come from?

Hands grabbed me and I gasped as I was pulled behind a pile of logs. I turned to find Damien kneeling beside me, his eyes searching the chaos erupting before us.

"Here, you'll need this," he said, handing me a snowball.

"Care to explain what exactly is going on?" I asked, a smile curving my lips.

Vincent directed children to aim at recruits taking shelter, ducking when a stray snowball was launched his way before throwing his in retaliation.

"It's one of our oldest traditions," Damien said, rising enough to hit Vincent in the arm before ducking back down. "The recruits bring their young, and Vincent or Barrett take them out to orchestrate a snowball fight."

"Come on," he said, nodding his head for me to join in. I looked over the logs to find Zephyr knelt behind his own cover, seeming not to realize we were here as he took aim elsewhere.

I threw the snowball as hard as I could, but it hit the ground in front of him. His head jerked in our direction, and I squeaked as I dropped back behind our cover.

"He saw me!" I whispered. Snow exploded against the top of our barricade, dusting us in bits of frost and ice as Zephyr retaliated.

Damien huffed a laugh. "Come on. He'll come looking for us; we need to change positions."

Damien rose just enough to throw a snowball at the children before grabbing my hand and pulling me elsewhere. Just as we reached another hiding spot, Barrett roared, and screams broke out as he popped up behind one of the children's barricades, scooping snow and throwing it over them. They scattered, their squeals and giggles filling the air, leaving my heart swelling.

"Come here!" Barrett yelled, chasing after them, only to be pelted with multiple snowballs.

The shadows converged beside me, and I fell to the side as five Lupai rose from their depths before leaping into a playful run. Their yips filled my ears as some ran to the children, tackling them to the ground to lick their faces. Laughter bubbled up my throat as one of them stuck its nose into a nearby snow pile before rolling around in it, its tongue falling out of its mouth in happiness.

"No!" a child shouted at the Lupai. "That's for snowballs!"

The Lupai twisted around to lick the child, its tongue so massive, it coated the entire side of her face in slobber as she giggled.

"Here," Damien said, placing another snowball in my hand before pointing at Thalia who had caught sight of us.

"How exactly does this work?" I asked, snowballs flying through the air in all directions.

"You get to pick a side. It's always been adults versus young, but you could do either side if you like," he explained.

"What determines the winner?"

"Usually, the war ends when one side surrenders, or if they're surrounded with no snow to fight back," he said with a chuckle. "Vincent is always with the children, as he uses water magic and can help them make more snow."

Movement caught my attention and I turned to find Thalia motioning for me to come to her. I glanced back at Damien briefly, and his brows furrowed.

"Good luck," I said before running through the fray toward Thalia.

CHAPTER 12
DAMIEN

I reached for Cassie as she made a dash for Thalia, but my hand clasped air, and I watched as she ran through the open expanse of the training yard, narrowly dodging snowballs as they flew through the air. She launched forward, narrowly avoiding getting hit, and slid on her side behind the barricade where Thalia had taken shelter. I narrowed my eyes, but a smile curved my lips as they began talking, likely hashing out a plan.

Our gazes met briefly, and her sneaky smile was all I needed to see to know she'd chosen her side... and I was one of her targets.

Then enemies we shall be, mea luna.

Zephyr appeared at my side, quickly getting to work converting the snow behind me into a stockpile of projectiles.

"I think Thalia's changing the game this year," I said, eyes narrowing as I caught sight of Sasha leaving Zach and Liam in favor of Cas and Thalia. The trio changed positions, chucking snowballs at Barrett and those at his side as they ran toward another female. Zephyr's brows rose, and he turned, pale green eyes following my line of sight as we watched their movements. They were gathering the other females, turning on the males at their side.

"A mutiny," Zephyr said, his lips curving into a smile before turning his sights to Barrett and whistling.

Barrett stopped mid-throw, his steel eyes shooting to us, and I nodded for him to join us. He hurried over, but not before chucking a snowball at one of the older children. They squealed, and he ducked under their fire to get to us.

"What's up?" he asked breathlessly as he knelt beside me, grabbing two of Zephyr's snowballs and throwing each in different directions.

"Hey, make your own," Zephyr growled.

"Thalia and Cas are changing the game," I said, nodding to them as their growing group divided in different directions. Sasha and another female attacked two unsuspecting males from behind, pelting them with snowballs until they surrendered.

"Little shits," Barrett muttered under his breath, but his eyes lit up as he watched them sweep across the training yard, capturing barricades and taking prisoners. Barrett grabbed another snowball from Zephyr's stash and rose quickly, chucking a snowball through the air and pelting Thalia in the side of the face.

She froze, eyes wide before she turned her attention to us.

"Now you've done it," Zephyr sighed as Thalia brushed the snow from her face and hair before a wicked smile curved her lips.

Barrett mouthed something to her, and I didn't have to know what it was exactly to know he was baiting her, inviting the all-out war brewing as Thalia turned the females against the males. She and Cassie didn't return Barrett's fire, instead running toward the group of children at Vincent's command, their hands held high.

"Shit," Zephyr breathed. "They're not doing what I think they're doing, are they?"

"They are," I said as I turned my gaze to Zach and Liam, who were currently waging their own battle with the two females Thalia, Sasha, and Cassie had left behind.

I whistled, and they twisted around, dropping to hide behind their barricade before looking my way. "The females are switching sides!"

They frowned, peering around the edge to where Thalia and Cassie were now smiling at Vincent. The children ran around Cassie, their smiles warming my chest, and a smile tugged at my lips at the sight of her own smile, of how she lit up as she helped them tighten their defenses.

"Traitor," Barrett breathed before throwing a snowball, which Vincent dodged.

"We're already down several of our own. Look," Zephyr said, nodding to the far side, where two females stood guard of six males who'd surrendered. "They'll have us outnumbered in no time, especially with Vincent and the young."

"We need to gather the others, free those captured, and launch an attack before they can organize their defenses," I said, looking between Barrett and Zephyr, who nodded.

"I'll take out the females guarding the others," Barrett said, a cocky grin on his face as he grabbed a few snowballs. "Then, we can regroup and take the females and children."

"Godsdammit, Barrett. You've wasted half of them! Aim better," Zephyr growled, moving what remained of his stockpile out of his reach.

"Why don't you actually throw them instead of stockpiling them?" Barrett bit back before grabbing another, and I wondered if it was just to spite him, which was confirmed when Barrett threw it without looking or aiming. "Is that a shifter thing? Do you bury your food too?"

Zephyr rolled his eyes before turning his back to him, blockading his snowy projectiles.

"Okay, you two. Barrett, you free the others," I said, turning my gaze from the chaos escalating quicker than normal. "Zephyr, you and I will move up the south side to draw their attention away, and Barrett you come up on their backs and—"

"Where'd Thalia go?" Zephyr asked with a frown, and my gaze shot toward where she'd been with Vincent and Cassie just a few moments before. Cassie was nowhere to be seen either. I began to count the young. Three. Four. When I got to six, I frowned.

"Barrett, weren't there twelve children today?" Barrett nodded and I let out a low sigh. "They're mobilizing. Thalia and Cassie must have slipped off with a group to do something. Watch your backs—"

Screams erupted at the far side as Thalia and three children emerged from the forest behind an unsuspecting duo of male recruits. The males shielded themselves as Thalia and the children pelted them with snowball after snowball until they were putting their hands up in surrender.

I couldn't help but laugh.

"Okay, no time for chatting. Get to it," I said as Barrett split away from us.

"I forgot how formidable Thalia is in warfare," Zephyr said. "Changing sides and forming a plan so quickly. I don't understand why she turned down the promotion you and Lucia offered her."

I remembered how her contributions to the war had saved countless lives, had helped us stabilize our forces long enough to bring Melantha down and turn the tables in our favor. I remembered the moment she'd turned us down—the title of third in command passed to Barrett instead and I remembered how he'd used that very position to pull her from patrols all those years ago to protect her. Did she regret her decision then? Did she regret it now?

"You think the young might actually win this year?" Zephyr asked as he watched Thalia take the two male prisoners to the others, the children giggling at her sides as they held snowballs ready to pelt them if they tried to run.

"Am I going to lose you to their side as well?" I asked, cocking a brow.

"Nope," he said, pressing a fist to his chest. "Can't get rid of me that easily. I've been at your side from the beginning, and that's where I'll remain until the end."

"So poetic for a snowball fight," I mused, and he laughed before gathering several snowballs in his arms. I grabbed some as well and we made our way down the perimeter. We paused periodically to throw snowballs at Vincent and the children, drawing their attention to us, and I caught sight of Barrett as he fell into position near the prisoners with two other males at his side, waiting for Thalia and those accompanying her to step away and leave the three females to guard them.

Screams, shouts, and laughter filled the air as both sides went after each other, snowballs continuing to sail through the air before splattering against faces, backs, and chests. Vincent called out orders to the children, turning attention in different directions as they moved forward, sliding into position behind new barriers, advancing on us now that our numbers were low.

"They're opening their backs for attack. Now's our chance," I said to Zephyr as I landed a hit against the side of Vincent's face, drawing his attention right where I wanted it. Zephyr ran south, getting into position to surround them as Barrett launched his assault on the unsuspecting females standing guard, their own battle erupting.

I threw another snowball and, as my will demanded, the five Lupai who'd been snorkeling and rolling in the snow turned their heads and charged for the children, sliding to a stop to lick their faces.

"That's cheating!" one of the children shouted with a giggle.

I huffed a laugh when the children became distracted by the shadow wolves as they pounced and ran around them, scattering and distracting them.

"I didn't think the King of Immortals would stoop to such lows," Cassie muttered, and I stiffened.

Before a storm of snowballs crashed into my back.

CHAPTER 13

CASSIE

Zephyr barked out a laugh as Damien recounted how three children and I ambushed him, taking him down before he knew what was happening. It wasn't long after we'd forced his surrender that Vincent had turned his attention on Zephyr. At the same time, Thalia and the others had rushed to aid the women—er… females—who'd been fighting to keep their prisoners against Barrett and the two males he'd recruited.

I curled up under the blanket, my bare feet laid out by the fire burning in the hearth at The Outpost. Almost all the recruits had left for the evening, taking the children with them after enjoying some much-needed hot cocoa. My boots had been soaked through by the time the fight was won, my toes and fingers numb, but it had been worth it to see the look on Damien's face when we'd caught him by surprise.

"Barrett let us down," Zephyr said, sliding an annoyed glance his way.

Barrett huffed. "Hey, you were supposed to hold them off long enough for me to take out the guards and release the others. You failed *me*!"

I snickered before pushing out my lower lip. "Poor babies."

"Easy for you to say, hiding away to avoid the battle instead of facing us head on," Barrett said as he ruffled his hand through my hair, and I batted his hand away.

"You're just upset we won," I taunted.

"You could've fought back," Barrett said, turning his gaze to Damien.

Damien looked as if he couldn't fathom the idea. "And crush the triumph in the eyes of the children?"

"Oh don't you downplay our victory," I said, narrowing my eyes at him, to which he threw his hands up. "We won fair and square. I'm not the one who sent five Lupai in to distract the children."

"I don't know what you're talking about," he said, becoming preoccupied with the marshmallows swimming in his cocoa. "They were just excited to play with the children."

"Sure," I drawled before rolling my eyes and taking a sip, groaning at the chocolatey warmth as it rolled down my throat.

Barrett and Damien started swapping stories of their own encounters during the snowball fight, and from the corner of my eye I caught sight of Zephyr's eyes falling to his phone, his onyx brows furrowing before he answered.

"What's up?" he whispered. His face hardened, pale green eyes widening before he rose and stalked toward the door.

Barrett and Damien didn't seem to take notice of him leaving as they fell deeper into their conversation, and I moved away, pulling the blanket tighter around me as I hurried toward the door where he'd disappeared. I slipped outside, the icy wind catching my hair, and I winced at the bite of frost beneath my bare feet. He disappeared around a corner, muttering something, and I followed after him, falling back behind the wall when he came to a stop before me. I stopped breathing, wondering if he'd seen me, but he didn't come back, and his voice reached my ears.

"What happened? Are you all right?" he asked, and I peeked around the corner to see a wrinkle forming between his eyebrows as he turned. I ducked back behind the wall before he could see me.

"Where are you?"

I pressed my back to the wall, guilt churning in my stomach for listening in on his conversation, but I was worried all the same. I should step out, should ask him what was wrong, if there was something I could do, but like a coward, I stayed hidden.

"Who?" His anger seared my skin, and I shivered at the intensity of it. My heart twisted. I'd never heard him so angry. What had happened? Who was he talking to?

"I want a fucking name," he growled. "Who put their hands on you?"

Oh God. Was someone hurt?

75

"Where are you? I'm coming to get you, now."

Shit. I turned, running back for the door at the sound of snow and mud squelching beneath his boots. I slipped back inside and closed the door, praying he hadn't caught me eavesdropping.

Damien's brows rose when I returned to his side, glancing over my shoulder to see if Zephyr would return, but he never did.

"Where'd you wander off to?" he asked, tilting his head.

"Oh, I was wondering where Zephyr disappeared to." It wasn't entirely untrue.

His brows furrowed, and he looked around. "That's a good question."

"I'm sure he's fine," I said, hoping that he was, and that the person he'd been speaking to was as well.

Damien ran a hand over his right arm, massaging it as his eyes drifted from me for a moment.

"You okay?" I asked, arching a brow. "Sore from getting your ass handed to you by children?"

He huffed a laugh. "I'll be fine. Selene's been trying to summon me for the past couple of weeks, and it's getting annoying."

My eyes flicked to his arm as he stretched it out before relaxing it again. It was the arm with the tattoo of his vows to Selene. "Does it hurt?"

"No. It's more of an annoyance if anything."

"Why don't you go to her?" I asked.

"I've just been busy, but I really should check in. I haven't given her any updates since we took out Marcus."

I hadn't realized it had been that long since he'd seen her. There were many times when work had pulled him away from me for many hours of the day, but I'd always assumed he visited her from time to time. Did he really dislike the goddess so much as to avoid her for this long despite her summons? Would he get in trouble?

"Come on," he said, groaning as he pushed himself to his feet. "*Mitera* will likely have dinner ready soon. We'll eat, and then I'll report to her."

"Will she be mad at you?" I asked, my brows wrinkling as he extended a hand to me.

He smiled warmly. "It'll be fine."

As he continued, his smile faded, his gaze leaving mine as annoyance painted his face. "She's likely just bored and wants me to entertain her with our *trivial* matters that have no effect on her whatsoever."

I nodded, taking his hand and rising to my feet. My eyes fell to the door where Zephyr had disappeared, and I hoped that whatever was happening, whoever he'd spoken to, he would be okay.

CHAPTER 14

DAMIEN

My feet met cold marble as I emerged from the void, the scent of jasmine filling my lungs. Pale moonlight leaking in through carvings in the ceiling of the temple painted my skin in its glow. It had been two weeks since I'd last set foot in this place, but I'd avoided facing Selene for too long—the nudge of her summons tingling in my vows to her, the ones inked in my skin.

When I lifted my eyes to her altar atop the dais, I blinked at the sight of it empty. The warhorse statues stood in quiet solitude without their master. My footsteps echoed through the empty hall as I stepped up the stairs, searching for any sign of the goddess. The halls were unusually bare. Normally they would be decorated for Winter Solstice. I remembered how beautifully Selene decorated the castle, our home, when I was young, how she would light up under the full moon's glow. Even if it wasn't the castle we'd once called home, the temple was a shadow of what it once was—cold and empty, and now even emptier than it had grown in the recent centuries.

As I came to a stop beside her altar, my eyes slid to one of the massive warhorses before me, their dormant power still felt despite their slumber.

"Hello, Arion, Arete. Where is she?" I asked, lifting a hand to press against the nose of one of the beasts who towered beyond any horse I'd ever seen, but of course they would. These were creatures of legend, beasts born of power and war.

Stone groaned, and Arion's head tilted into my touch, his eyes lighting up as he awoke from his slumber. Hot breath spilled over me as the creature exhaled before turning its gaze to the single door at the back of the dais leading to Selene's private chambers.

Something in the way the ink in my skin chilled left me uneasy. I couldn't place it, but it almost felt familiar. She rarely summoned me, content in her solitude, her sprites and warhorses seeming to be enough company for her.

I hesitated before tapping my knuckle against the ancient wood door, adorned with intricate carvings of a massive glowing dimós tree with a depiction of the deity Celestia curved over the top, tears rolling down her cheeks before falling to the earth below, where the dimós trees sprouted and grew.

"Selene?"

There was no response, and I glanced back at the two horses, who watched me silently. I knocked once more. "Apologies for disturbing you at this hour, Goddess. It's Damien."

Still no response. It would be like her to be upset that I hadn't given her the time she felt entitled to, but before I could write her off, I stiffened as a thought crossed my mind. Was she unwell? I couldn't remember ever seeing the goddess fall ill or refuse my visits or... I paused, remembering when I'd gone to her to beg her to help with Emilia, only to find her locked away in her chambers after Lucia had passed away.

I frowned, searching the room for a sign of anything that might have happened, but nothing stood out. The dimós trees cast their warm glow as they always did, bare branches stretching out toward the high ceilings where the night sky and her stars were trapped. Arion and Arete remained at her altar, eyes still lingering on me, unable to move from where they stood.

"I shall return another time," I said, turning to head back down the stairs of the dais. She was likely just upset with me for avoiding her summons.

As I stepped into the void, though, I couldn't help but feel like something might be wrong.

CHAPTER 15
CASSIE

I stared into eyes of a lost past on the easel before me. Eyes that were once my own had been brought back to life in a rough sketch I had been working on all afternoon. It was almost done and ready for watercolors, something I never imagined I would ever touch again.

My sleep had been filled with pleasant dreams for once. No, not dreams—memories. Memories I'd longed to experience.

"I told you it would be the perfect tree," I said, beaming as I tucked one final pinecone into place among the ornaments we'd crafted or collected over the years: stained pine cones, sticks of cinnamon and dried chaza berries Damien had brought home from the Godsrealm—the berries a sweet remembrance of his mother and the desserts she made for us as children—a few carved wood pieces Zephyr had gifted me over the years, and strands of yarn decorated with wooden beads I'd spent the past few weeks carving and refining until they were just right to string around the tree.

I glanced back at Damien, my smile so wide, my cheeks were growing sore. My heart fluttered at the warmth of his gaze as he watched me from the other side of the tree where he'd placed another ornament.

"You're always right," he said, and I realized his hand was behind his back.

I cocked an eyebrow, my eyes narrowing. "What're you hiding?"

One corner of his lips curved into a crooked grin, and he pulled a small box from his back, tied together with delicate ivory ribbon. My eyes lit up as I stepped toward him.

A tag dangled from the ribbon with my name written across it. Elena.

"I found it on my last trip to the Godsrealm and I thought of you." He held it out to me. "Open it."

I reluctantly took the box, fingers hovering over the ribbon as my eyes lifted to him. "But I haven't gotten your Solstice gift yet."

He shook his head. "This isn't your Solstice gift. Don't worry about that. This is just something extra."

I looked back down at the box before running my fingers over the silk ribbon. It was so beautiful, so soft, and I tugged it loose before removing the lid. My eyes widened, breath rushing from my lungs at what I saw.

Nestled within a bed of glittering silk was a crystal. Not just any crystal — this was carved with the most detail I'd ever seen. It was a creature of legend, one I'd know anywhere. The Eternis Moth was a beloved creature, companion to the deity, Celestia. There was only one to have ever existed in the history of the Godsrealm, and stories told of its size, far larger than any moth on either side of the veil, its massive wings tipped with delicate teardrop shaped tails. Whoever had made the crystal neglected no detail, including the phases of the moon on the creature's wings, which represented the endless cycles of rebirth the creature underwent.

Damien stepped to my side to look down at the delicate ornament. "When I visited Belimus to meet with Zeus, I came across a Lapidarist in the market, working on the most intricately cut crystals. They were the most beautiful things I'd ever seen, and when I saw this, I remembered how much you loved The Eternis Moth, how often you'd ask my mother to tell you stories of it at bedtime so many centuries ago."

The familiarity of it tugged at something deep in my chest, a part of me long lost, rising to the surface as if summoned at the mere memory of it. It had always been my favorite story, in this life and the last.

"I don't know what to say," I said, tears dotting my eyelashes. "It's beautiful."

He pressed a kiss to my temple as he ran his fingers through my blonde hair. "Why don't we put it on the tree?"

"I think that's a wonderful idea," I said, taking the ribbon that had tied the box together, and running it through the loop before tying it.

I lifted my gaze to the yew tree, and as if it were meant to be, my eyes found a place, a gap in the ornaments I hadn't noticed. I pushed myself up, hooking the *ribbon over some of the needles. The crystal caught the firelight as I stepped back to admire it, the facets of the carved surface near glittering as it gently swayed before settling in place.*

Damien's arms came around me, pulling me closer against him as he pressed his face into my neck, inhaling deeply. My eyes caught sight of a nearby mirror. His dark hair fell over my blonde, my silver eyes near glowing in the dimly lit room as the flickering candlelight reflected in them.

The sound of the front door opening echoed through the house, and I stiffened, turning my attention from the easel to the open doorway of my library.

"Cas? Damien?" Barrett called, and I set my charcoal down before rising.

"Barrett?" I responded, wiping my hands on a damp rag to clean the smudges of charcoal coating my fingertips. He entered the living room, Thalia behind him, and I frowned at the two large boxes in his arms.

"Hey, spitfire!"

I blinked and looked back at the hallway behind him. "I could've sworn the front door was locked."

"Yeah, about that," he said with a shit-eating grin. "I knew he wouldn't find the time to decorate—he never does. Figured we'd get to work, with it only being ten days away."

Shit. I hadn't been able to get something for Damien yet. I wondered if Kat had finished midterms so we could go shopping.

Ethel appeared in the hallway. "Barrett, we already have décor fer the house."

"I thought I'd contribute," he said, setting his boxes down on the couch before looking around and frowning. "You guys haven't picked out a tree yet?"

I cocked an eyebrow. "We've sort of been busy."

"Where the hell is Damien?" he asked, looking around.

"Meeting with Selene. I'm not sure when he'll be back," I said, walking over to see what he brought.

"Did he talk to you about Solstice yet?"

"No," I said, eyeing him.

He let out a groan before flopping on the couch. "Gods, he's slacking."

"Give him a break. He's got a lot he's overseeing."

"And a lot he's cleanin' up with ye gettin' intae trouble," Ethel grumbled, propping a hand on her hip.

Barrett gave her a guilty grin. "I wouldn't be getting into so much trouble if I wasn't taking care of stuff outside The Order, as he asked me to."

I tilted my head, brows furrowing.

"I guess we could start decorating the living room," he said before I could pry, and he began pulling strings of garland from the box. The scent of yew hit me hard, and I stepped closer, ready to help if I could.

"What's going on here?" Damien asked as Barrett and I started running the garland over the mantel.

I jumped, turning around to find him leaning against the cased opening to the hallway, arms crossed over his chest with a smug smile on his lips, one dark brow cocked.

"Figured we'd pick up the slack," Barrett said, not sparring him a glance. "Can't have a Solstice celebration without decorations, and this house is still entirely too depressing for the season."

Damien's eyes narrowed. "It's not depressing in here."

Thalia snickered from where she and Ethel hung garland along the bay window.

"It is for this time of year," Barrett argued.

Damien shook his head, and opened his mouth, but Barrett cut him off. "Spitfire, Damien wanted to know if you'd join us for Solstice this year."

My gaze snapped to Barrett before turning back to Damien, who let out a sigh but turned his nervous gaze to me.

I hesitated. "I..."

"I've been meaning to ask you, but I wasn't sure if you would prefer to spend it with your parents," Damien said, his brows wrinkling as he stepped toward me. "I know you miss them, so I was unsure whether you'd choose to spend the holidays with us or them. I didn't want to make you choose."

"Of course I'd love to spend Solstice with you," I said as he approached. "I just wasn't sure what the traditions were, if it would be strange for a human to participate."

His eyes softened, and he cupped my cheek. "I couldn't imagine celebrating it again without you, human or immortal."

My heart squeezed at his words, and I smiled.

"It's gonna be a party," Barrett said, his eyes lighting up. "Every year, we do a gift exchange, and everyone is assigned a random person. Then we do all kinds of things, and then *Mitera* cooks us a delicious dinner, and—"

"Down, boy," Thalia said, cutting him off before turning to me with a warm smile. "Ignore him. He's just excited to celebrate it with you."

My smile widened into a grin. "It sounds like fun."

"I thought you might invite your parents to join us for dinner on Solstice. Kat's welcome too if she doesn't have plans," Damien offered.

I blinked, my heart launching into my throat at the thought of my parents. I'd spoken to Mom off and on over the past couple of weeks about Christmas, and while they had offered for me to come, I'd been undecided, but I hadn't talked to Dad much at all since our last fight. Maybe this could help smooth things out. "Okay. I think that would be a great idea. I was actually talking to Kat and her parents won't be back to celebrate with her."

"She's as much family as my brothers and their mates are," he said with a smile that warmed me down to my toes. "I'd love for her to join us."

"Well, first things first. We need a tree," Barrett said before looking past me to Damien. "We doin' this the old fashioned way?"

"Ethel's been buying trees, but I think it would be nice to do it as we used to," Damien said before his gaze drifted to me, his eyes warm.

"Is that because I always pick the perfect tree?" I asked with a knowing smile, and his eyes widened just a fraction, his smile fading.

"Did you..." he started but couldn't seem to ask.

"I had a flicker of a memory resurface before the snowball fight last week, and last night I dreamt of a Solstice with you." My eyes drifted as the images danced in my thoughts, of the sight of him holding me in the mirror. It had all felt so perfect. "We were decorating a tree in our cottage on the outskirts of Moonhaven."

He took my hands in his, lifting them to press a kiss to my knuckles. "Let's go pick the perfect tree, then."

CHAPTER 16

DAMIEN

"Gods, I feel like this might be the biggest tree you've ever picked," I groaned as Barrett and I dragged it up the back porch steps, the sun making its final descent behind the mountains surrounding the valley.

"Are you sure? The tree I saw in my dream looked just as tall," Cassie said, a wrinkle forming between her brows as she and Thalia followed close behind us.

Ethel turned our way, gray brows rising as we lugged the tree through the kitchen door, bits of dirt and snow littering the wood floors as we went. She let out a sigh, placing her hand on her hip. "Now Ah'll have tae mop again."

"Worth it, though!" Barrett said, his smile wide with delight. "Look at this tree Cas picked out!"

Her eyes lit up as she took a moment to look it over. "Oh mah goodness. I daresay that's the biggest tree we've had in ages."

"I don't know. What if it's too big?" Cassie said, her chestnut brows wrinkling as she watched from the doorway. "I hope you guys didn't drag it up here just for it not to fit."

"It'll fit," I said, focusing on not crashing the trunk into the wall as we carried it into the hallway toward the living room. "You've never picked wrong."

She didn't seem convinced. "We'll see."

Barrett and I got it into the tree stand before lifting it up. Cassie watched from where she stood nearby with Thalia, hands over her mouth, as if she were afraid what she said might be true. We got it into place, and the top of the tree almost brushed the ceiling. Cassie let out a breath of relief, and I chuckled.

"It's perfect," I said, glancing back at her as I pulled my coat off, the sight of her warm smile enough to undo me. It was genuine, one I wished I could see on her face every day.

"We'll get started on the other stuff," Barrett said, and he and Thalia started pulling garland and other pieces from the storage bins.

"I think you should place the first ornament," I said, reaching into our bin, searching for a specific one.

She tilted her head as she stepped closer, curiosity lighting those beautiful hazel eyes.

I pulled the little black box from the bubble wrap. It had seen better days, the corners frayed, edges worn down, but what lay inside the box was just as perfect as it had been when I'd first brought it home to her.

Her lips parted the moment she saw it.

"Here," I said, holding it out to her.

She hesitated a moment before she took the box from my hand. "Is this..."

I nodded, and her eyes lit up before she lifted the lid. For a moment, I saw Elena standing before me, beaming like she had when I'd given her the ornament. Lucia's eyes had lit up the same way when I'd presented it to her our first Solstice together after I found her again. Time could stop, and I almost wished it would, just so I could be lost in this moment with her.

Tears dotted her eyes as she reached into the box and looped her fingers into the ivory ribbon she'd tied to it over seven hundred years ago. Time had left no marks on the carved crystal, the etchings of crescent moons and delicate swirls of the wings glittering still.

She lifted the ornament, allowing it to dangle from her fingers, the crystal coming to life in the fire's glow. "It's as beautiful as I remember it," she whispered, a single tear rolling down her cheek.

I stepped closer to her, pressing a kiss to her forehead as she ran her hand over her cheek, brushing away the tear. "Anywhere?"

I nodded to the tree. "Wherever you like."

As she hung the ornament, the front door opened, and I turned to see Zephyr, James, Vincent, and Anna enter the living room a few moments later.

"Sorry we're late," Vincent said, rubbing his hands together as he stepped into the living room. "It took us a bit longer to finish packing the harvest for The Order's celebration."

"Sorry about that," Anna said sheepishly. "I misjudged the timing."

"I didn't know you were supposed to be here at a certain time," I muttered before my eyes slid to Barrett. "Didn't even know any of you were coming tonight."

"What?" Barrett said, feigning innocence while Anna snickered. "We've gotta pick names for Solstice, and you've been dragging your feet on preparations."

"Pick a name?" Cassie asked as I opened my mouth to retort.

"Barrett is overseeing the gift exchange," Vincent explained. "We pick a name and that's who we gift."

"Oh, that's right, I forgot you mentioned that," Cassie said.

"Since everyone's here, let's get that knocked out and then we'll finish decorating," Barrett said as he grabbed something from one of the boxes he'd brought.

"Okay, Damien, since you're hosting this year, you're first," he said, holding out the small box full of folded slips of papers.

"You're hosting?" Cassie asked, brows rising.

"*We're* hosting," I said, smiling down at her. "Why did you think we were decorating?"

"I don't know," she said, clearly flustered, her cheeks turning a faint shade of pink. "People like to decorate for the holidays. I thought it was just a thing."

I pulled her closer to me. "This is our home now, and I'd love nothing more than to celebrate the end of the season with you at my side."

A soft smile tugged at her lips. "I'd love that."

My heart soared at the sight of her smile, at the fact that she was accepting the invitation to be with us—our family nearly whole once again.

Barrett held the box out to me, and I reached inside, grabbing the first piece of paper I felt. He then went around the room, holding out the box to everyone as they took their own slip of paper.

"Spitfire?" he said, turning to her. She rolled her eyes but grabbed a piece of paper, and Barrett grabbed the last one. "Okay, open 'em up."

I unfolded my paper just as everyone else did, smiling when I saw Cassie's name written out in Barrett's scratchy handwriting.

I guess you won't be getting her lingerie after all.

"Who'd you get?" Cassie asked.

"I can't tell you that," I said coyly. "That ruins the fun of it."

She rolled her eyes and started toward Thalia. "Thalia."

Cassie leaned in, cupping her hands over her mouth as she whispered something in Thalia's ear, and for a brief moment, Thalia's eyes flickered to me before a smile crept across her face.

Cassie pulled away, and my brows furrowed as she whispered. "Do you think you could do that?"

Thalia nodded. "I think I can manage that. It's the right time of year."

Cassie's eyes lit up.

Barrett huffed a laugh as he unfolded his, pulling my attention from Cassie and Thalia, and I cocked an eyebrow. He shook his head. "You'll find out on Solstice."

CHAPTER 17
CASSIE

My grip slipped, and I yelped as I slid down the face of the mountainside before my fingers wedged into a small crack in the rocks. I groaned at the bite of the stone scraping against my knees and forearms as I slid to a stop.

"Cas!" Damien cried out from the ledge above where he and other recruits had gathered.

"I'm okay!" I gasped as I dangled, my shoulders burning from the climb, my fingers—nearly my entire body—slippery with mud.

Fuck!

My heart raced as I reached for another edge of rock jutting from the stone face, simultaneously finding a place for my boot to help support my weight.

Don't look down. Don't fucking look down!

I lifted my gaze to the last five feet separating me from the top. I still hadn't found the strength to reach the top of the rock wall—this particular obstacle thwarting me the past three times we'd practiced this course—and the distance seemed to taunt me once more.

My teeth ground together as I pulled myself up, reaching for the next piece of rock I could fit my fingers into. I could do this. I *would* do this. There was only one more obstacle beyond this, and then I'd have beaten this course, despite the odds.

It had been nearly two weeks since I'd first taken a shot at this course. My stamina had improved since I'd started my training, and while I was still struggling to keep up with the others, the pace I'd set for myself didn't seem to aggravate my heart. There were times where I had to stop, my limits keeping me from pushing myself as hard as I'd like, but hope had risen in my chest with each day.

I was getting stronger. Faster.

This was my fourth attempt, and I refused to let myself fall short again, even if I was completing it far slower than the other recruits.

I grunted as my shoulders protested under my weight, my fingers burning from the scrape of rock. My gaze shot to the ledge, growing closer and closer, until—

"Shit," I panted, my eyes darting over the remaining gap of space. This was always where I got stuck. My arms were too short to reach the next ledge, and I'd been too tired to hold myself in my last attempt. My mind flew to that first time, when I'd fallen.

There was nothing like a hard fall to make you hesitate, but I refused to let it defeat me.

You're human. These training courses were designed for immortals whose bodies are built differently from yours. You can't approach it like they do. You have to get creative.

Damien's words flitted through my mind. I ground my teeth, stretching my hand out, but my fingers fell short, and I cursed under my breath. There was no other way. If I lingered anymore my grip would slip and this would be another failed attempt.

"Come on, Cas!" Zephyr called from Damien's side, and I steeled my nerves, drowning out the fear, and kicked off. The world went quiet, my heart faltering as I reached out, gravity threatening to tear me down. I grunted as my fingers wedged into the crevice amidst the rocks.

Shit, shit!

My arm buckled under my weight, and I desperately threw my free hand out for the ledge before me, barely catching the stony surface. I cried out in relief before pulling myself up, my body fighting me every inch until I was throwing my leg over the edge onto solid ground. I collapsed on the pathway, my hands and arms trembling as I panted.

The recruits broke into a chorus of cheers and shouts as I tried to find the will to get up.

One more obstacle. Can't stop now.

I forced myself to my feet, my legs weak. Small rocks slipped from beneath my boots and rolled down the steep slope to the ground below as I stood, trying to regain my bearings. God, I was exhausted, my heart racing.

So close. I was so fucking close I could almost taste it as I lifted my gaze to the next obstacle. My boot slipped on the rock as I pushed myself up, the exhaustion wearing me down, and my hands shot out as I narrowly caught myself against the steep, slick, stony path up the mountain, my knees trembling, my body exhausted. I panted, my throat dry, icy air burning my lungs.

"You've got this, Cas!" Vincent called out from below.

"Don't give up; you're almost there!" Sasha shouted, cheering me on as she, Zach, and Liam watched amidst the small crowd of recruits, waiting for their turn to complete the course.

I came to a stop at the top of the path, and my eyes fell on the gap a few feet ahead of me: the last obstacle I needed to clear to complete the course. It was symbolic of the gaps between rooftops we would have to clear while on patrol. It was easily six feet, and my heart plummeted as I fought the urge to let my gaze fall to the thirty-foot drop if I missed. It wouldn't be a free fall, but the roll down the mountainside would be painful, to say the least. I'd watched the recruit before me crash into the ledge when he misjudged the distance and rolled down the mountainside. He'd broken a few ribs and was being seen by the medic stationed at The Outpost.

"You're holding up the line," Aiden called from below, his arms folded across his broad chest as he watched with a bored expression. I ignored him, not sure why he was so impatient—it wasn't as if he was running the course.

"Don't be such a dick!" Sasha said, elbowing him, to which he gave her warning glare.

"Ignore him, Cas. You've got this!" Damien shouted from across the gap, his worried eyes locked on me. A smile curved my lips at how, despite his worry, he let me do this on my own. He never held me back despite my limitations, always pushed me forward. I loved that about him, appreciated it more than I could put into words.

Icy air burned my lungs as I paused for a breath, bracing myself against my knees.

You can do this. Just don't fucking look down!

I readied myself as I stood at the very edge of the run. With maybe four or five feet of path before me, there wasn't much room to get a good running start, but immortals didn't need as much of a start as a human would. They were designed for this—stronger, faster. All of them came into recruitment training stronger than I was, even after the weeks of training I'd endured. It was infuriating.

Can you handle a second fall? The voice slithered across my thoughts.

"And here I was thinking I'd finally get some peace and quiet," I muttered, trying not to let fear take root.

"Don't second guess it!" Damien said from the other side, and I didn't miss the look of fear in his eyes. "Hesitation gets you killed in the field!"

He was right. I couldn't hesitate, couldn't second guess. I was done second guessing myself. No more delaying. I drew a deep breath and leapt into a run, pebbles and rocks crunching and slipping beneath my boots as I sprinted for the gap. It seemed to stretch, growing impossibly wider than I could possibly jump as I drew closer, and my heart fell into the pit of my stomach.

I couldn't do this. I couldn't do this. Shit, I was going to fall.

"Don't stop!" Damien shouted, taking a step forward, his eyes widening.

My heart stuttered, my boot hitting the stone path one final time before I pushed through the fear and leapt. Wind rushed around me, and I gasped as I went airborne, my arms stretching out, as if I could somehow propel myself forward.

Shit. Shit!

Air burst from my lungs as I slammed into the ledge, narrowly avoiding my ribs crashing into the edge. I grunted as I scrambled to get ahold of something, anything, but my fingers only slipped on the solid stone, smaller rocks breaking free of the path and failing me. No matter what I did, my fingers slipped, the rocks slick from the morning dew. Fuck, why did we do this when everything was fucking wet? A gasp burst from my lips as I slid farther, unable to find anything solid. I was going to fall. Oh God, I was going to fall.

No. No. No!

My arms folded over the edge, my teeth gritting together as I managed to get a grip. A cacophony of shouts erupted below me as the other recruits cheered me on.

Damien took a step forward but held himself in place, his jaw clenching as he watched. He couldn't help; I *wouldn't* let him help. I'd made that clear before we started this course: I would complete it on my own, and only when I failed could he intervene.

My boots scraped across the stone as I fought to pull myself up, and Damien drew a sharp breath as my grip slipped once more, but I narrowly caught myself. I grunted as I found a space in the rock to wedge my toe into, and I climbed up and over the ledge before collapsing onto my back as I drew in deep breaths.

Damien and Zephyr rushed to my side, sliding to their knees as they checked me over.

"I did it," I panted, a smug grin tugging at my lips, my chest heaving. "I..." I drew another deep gasp. "I did it."

"You fucking did it," Damien said, pride lighting his eyes as he held out his hand to help me up.

"I thought we'd be rushing you to the medic, *again*," Zephyr admitted as we walked through the forest after our lunch break. "I think I stopped breathing when you almost fell from that ledge."

I huffed a laugh. "It wasn't like I would've died."

The nervous look he slid my way made it seem as if he hadn't been so sure.

"Caleb fell and he was fine," I added.

"Caleb's immortal," he said. "You're not built like us."

"Way to remind me of my weaknesses," I grumbled, crossing my arms over my chest as I turned my gaze from him.

"Sorry," he muttered before he drew a deep breath. "I'm proud of you, really. What you did today is nothing short of amazing. Almost half of the *immortal* recruits didn't complete the course, yet you, a human, managed to complete it."

"I also completed it with the slowest time," I muttered.

"You *completed* it," he said firmly, tilting his head as I rolled my eyes. "You don't give yourself enough credit. You've only been training for a month now."

"We don't exactly have the luxury of time, though," I said, my arms falling to my side. "The darklings. Melantha. Cole. They could strike at any time. I need to get stronger, faster. I want..."

He arched an onyx brow.

"I want to be at Damien's side when he's out hunting darklings. I want to hunt them myself." I wanted to hunt Cole and drag him back to pry any secrets or knowledge he may have about Melantha and the darklings from his mind.

How delicious it would be to taste his pain, to make him bleed.

An unsettling feeling sank into my bones as the venomous words slithered through my thoughts, and I wasn't sure if I could bring myself to disagree. Would I really find pleasure in his pain?

Zephyr let out a heavy sigh. "You'll get there. We're expecting this group to start shadowing in the field mid-January."

I stiffened. "Really? Would I—"

"You would be among them," he said, seeming to already know I'd ask. "Damien hasn't mentioned it to you?"

I shook my head. "I know he's not thrilled about it. He's had a lot on his mind lately, and when we get time alone he tries not to bring up work if he can help it."

He gave me an apologetic smile. "He's been pulling a lot of hours."

"I'm worried about him."

He lifted his hand to press his finger between my furrowed brows and flashed me a teasing grin. "Stop that. You'll be stuck with a permanent frown if you keep at it."

I pulled away from him, unable to hide the smile he too easily pulled from me.

He laughed, and we fell back into step as we continued through the forest toward the clearing for training. Sadly, I'd failed to shift, but at the end of our last session, something had felt different, and I was eager to try again.

"Solstice is only a few days away. Are you ready for it?" he asked, tilting his head.

"I think so." I had managed to sneak away with Kat to go shopping a few days ago. "I hope Damien likes what I got him."

"Did you get him for the gift exchange?"

I shook my head. "No, I got Barrett. I found something I think he'll like. It's nothing special, though."

"I'm sure they'll love their gifts, whatever they are."

He briefly pulled his phone from his pocket, his pale green eyes falling to the screen before typing a quick message and shoving it back into his pocket. It was hard to miss the awkward glance he shot my way before his gaze fell to the forest before us.

Guilt churned in my gut as I remembered listening in on his conversation a few days prior. I couldn't help but wonder if it was the same person he was texting.

"I..."

Zephyr's brows rose as he glanced at me.

"I have to tell you something," I admitted, and then the words flew from my mouth. "I want you to understand, I didn't mean to do it. It just sort of happened. I was worried about you, and then you were talking, and I wanted to step out and check on you, but then you got so angry, I—"

He placed a hand on my shoulder. "Cas, calm down, it's all right. Just tell me what happened."

"I overheard your phone call the other day," I said, my eyes falling from his. Fuck. I hoped he wouldn't be, but he'd have every right to be pissed at me.

He frowned, blinking, as if trying to recall what I was talking about.

"After the snowball fight," I clarified. "You stormed outside, and I followed, worried that something was wrong."

He drew a deep breath, running his fingers through his hair.

"I'm so, so sorry," I said, grimacing as I imagined how angry he might get with me. "I didn't mean to listen in on your conversation. I just didn't know how to approach you after you got angry."

"Sorry I scared you like that," he said, sliding a glance my way, and my steps slowed at the unmistakable balmy, icky feeling of guilt over my skin. Guilt? Why would he feel guilty?

"You don't have to answer, but... is your friend okay?" I asked, tilting my head to look up at him.

"She's all right," he said.

"Is she a friend of yours? Do I know her?"

"I guess you could say that," he hedged. "It's...complicated."

I nodded, not wanting to press him further. It was enough to know the situation had been handled, and that everything was, for the most part, okay.

"You seem to have gotten to know more of the recruits in the past couple of weeks," Zephyr said as we neared the edge of the clearing.

"All but one it seems," I said, catching onto his eagerness to change the subject.

His brows furrowed. "Who?"

"Aiden. He seems... I don't know, annoyed with me?" I bit my lip as a smile forced its way across my face. "Damien looked like he was about ready to go off on him when he made that comment about me holding up the line."

"Aiden's worse than Barrett sometimes," Zephyr said, annoyance painting his words. "He's a powerful warrior and has become quite the asset to The Order, but I swear, the guy is the epitome of his magic. All fire and rage."

"I'm honestly afraid to even talk to him."

"Stay away from him," Zephyr warned. "He's got zero patience, and he's been reprimanded for losing his temper and hurting others in the past."

Unease settled into the pit of my stomach. Why was he still around with a track record like that? I guess we were desperate with the numbers Damien had given me. We'd managed to gain a few new recruits since I'd joined, but it still wasn't enough.

"But enough about him. We're here to practice shifting," Zephyr said, coming to a stop.

I perked up at his words. "You want me to just continue what we've been trying?"

He nodded. "You've been studying the owl you want to shift into, right?"

96

"Yeah." Damien had gotten me a book on birds with great images of the barn owl, and I'd been studying every last detail of it, committing everything to memory.

"Perfect. Now, just focus on those details, just like we discussed before."

Air filled my lungs as I drew a deep breath, and I closed my eyes, focusing.

Talons instead of toes.

Nothing.

Wings instead of arms.

My skin tingled, something building in my chest, but I didn't break my concentration.

Feathers over my skin.

I imagined the bird in my mind, its mottled tawny feathers, dusted with whites and grays. I imagined its massive black eyes, its sharp talons used to snatch up prey.

Zephyr remained quiet, but I frowned as something strange passed over me, wind kissing my skin before sending ripples of a tingling energy over me. I gasped as a sinking sensation dragged me down.

"Don't panic. You've got it," Zephyr said, and my eyes shot open.

For a moment, I blinked, then tilted my head as I realized I was staring at Zephyr's knees. I lifted my eyes to find him towering over me, and I stumbled back, a screech peeling from my lips.

I froze. Not lips—a beak. I opened and closed my beak, the click satisfying as I looked down over myself, over the tawny feathers dusted in flecks of white and gray, just as I had imagined them.

"You did it!" Zephyr shouted before kneeling to my level.

"Holy shit!" I breathed, twisting around to look at myself, my wings fanning out awkwardly as I stumbled. "Oh my god, I can't believe that sound came out of me."

He barked a laugh. "I didn't mean to startle you."

"I can't believe I actually did it!" I shouted, my wings flying out on their own in my excitement, beating in the wind and kicking up bits of snow and dirt.

"Slow down. No flying today," he said, holding his hands out as my wings sagged to the ground.

"Well you're no fun," I groaned.

"Trust me. Flying isn't easy, but if you can master this, you'll be able to master any form."

I lifted one of my feet—er, talons—inspecting the sharp claws as I flexed and stretched them. "I guess I'd better start getting used to this body so you can teach me how to fly, then."

He huffed a laugh. "As impatient as always."

CHAPTER 18

CASSIE

"Thank you so much, *Mitera*," I said as I set the tray out on the counter to cool, feeling confident in the final touches I'd placed on the first gift for Damien.

Ethel smiled in that motherly way she always did, but there was something different this morning. She'd watched, helping me prep and work all morning with something akin to adoration. "Ah'll keep an eye on them."

"If he comes down without me, don't let him see," I pleaded as I backed toward the hallway.

She winked. "He'll have tae throw me out of the way tae get tae these."

I snickered and turned to hurry down the hall and up the stairs to our room. I'd snuck out while Damien was still asleep to begin working a couple of hours ago, and the sun had risen in the time it took to finish it. His other gift was tucked away in my library, awaiting tonight's celebration.

Damien had a rough patrol the night before, with darkling encounters at all three sectors. When he finally got home—later than usual—he'd been exhausted, covered in blood from head to toe. Despite the odds no one had been lost or severely injured. He'd taken Solstice off, leaving the shifts to volunteers who were all right working for extra pay, and I'd never been more relieved for him to take a break.

I cracked our door open to find him still curled up under the blankets, and my heart swelled at the sight of him, of his face so soft and peaceful in sleep. Then, my eyes started to wander, down over his exposed chest, further over the ripple of muscle across his abdomen, to the deep V that disappeared into his sweatpants.

Heat washed over me.

There had been few nights we hadn't wound up tangled up in each other in the last month. Anna had warned me of the effects of the mating bond, but I hadn't expected them to be so strong—the pull to be so consuming. He was insatiable at times—for my body, my blood. But at the same time, I couldn't get enough of him either. The need to feel his skin against mine, feel his lips, his body, to feel him inside me, consumed me. I couldn't have resisted even if I wanted to.

The mere thought of it left my body hungry for him, my skin heating as I thought of all the ways he'd taken me in this bed, the shower, this room.

I tiptoed toward him and eased onto the bed, leaning over to gaze at his beautiful face. He'd shaved a few days before, the stubble I loved so much already growing back in. A loose curl slipped over my shoulder, and I tucked it back into place behind my ear before I brushed my lips against his, his skin soft against mine.

He inhaled, and I smiled as his lips moved against mine. I broke the kiss to find the amber in his ashen eyes near glowing as he gazed up at me, as if gazing at a sky full of starlight.

"Good morning, *mea sol*," I whispered, lingering within a breath's distance of his lips, before giving him another tender kiss.

"Good morning, *mea luna*," he echoed, his voice rough as his lips pulled back into the sweetest smile. He lifted his hand to comb his fingers through my curls, and I tilted my head into the touch, the sensation sending goosebumps skittering over my skin.

His hand slid over my shoulder where my loose sweater had slid down to expose skin, around to my back, and then lower before he pulled me down onto him. A laugh burst from my lips as he pulled me down onto his chest.

He peppered kisses over my cheek, down my neck, wherever he could place them until I was squirming, unable to hold the laughter at bay at the way his stubble tickled my skin. He rolled us over until I was beneath him, his naked body pressing me into the mattress, and my breath hitched at the feel of him hard against me.

His lips crashed into mine, his tongue sweeping in to taste me, and I moaned into him as he rocked his hips against me, stoking the flame that had already started to light at the sight of him in our bed.

My hands shot up, tangling in his dark waves as I pulled him closer, deepening the kiss, needing more of him, something deep within me calling out, desperate to feel him closer. He slid his hands up under my sweater, pulling it up to expose my breasts. A moan burst from my lips as he dipped down to nip at the exposed flesh, his tongue flicking against the taught peak before he drew it between his teeth.

His eyes lifted to me as he sucked and teased, and my breath hitched as his hand slid between us, down into my underwear.

"So wet for me," he breathed against my skin and my back bowed as he ran his finger down my center, feeling every inch of the heat building inside me.

A moan burst from me as he brushed his thumb over the bundle of nerves that was throbbing, aching to be touched, before he sank a finger deep inside me. My head fell back, lips parting as a gasp burst from my throat. He watched me with hungry eyes as he pumped his fingers in and out, devouring the sight of me writhing beneath him. His fingers slid out, and I fell into a panting mess on the blankets, lifting my eyes to his as he drew his finger between his lips, tasting me.

"Gods, you taste divine."

He peeled my underwear down my legs before tossing them to the floor. I pushed myself up, and he settled back, allowing me room as my lips collided with his. My tongue swept in as my hands roamed over his chest, tasting him, tasting me. There was something unmistakably right about it, about the way he felt against me.

I broke the kiss just long enough to pull my sweater over my head before my lips were against his again. A satisfied hum rippled from his throat as I grabbed his arms, guiding him down onto his back. He watched me with curious eyes as I straddled him, but as I ran my fingers down his hard length, his eyes slid shut, hands fisting in the blankets. I lifted myself, watching his lips part in a silent moan as I slid down onto him, and my head fell forward as he stretched me, as I absorbed every inch of him until I was panting.

"Fuck, Cas," he growled before his hands found my hips.

I planted my hands on his chest before I rocked my hips forward, and a moan slipped past my lips. His eyes opened, just slightly, as he guided my hips, dragging me back and forth against him. My back arched at the angle, at the feel of him deep inside me. God, it felt good—too good.

He rose, his hand wrapping around the back of my neck to drag me down to him as he bit down on my throat, fangs slicing into my skin before pleasure shot up my spine, my back arching as I stilled.

"Don't you fucking stop," he growled, breaking his connection just long enough to speak. "I want to feel you come all over me."

He bit down again, and I did as he asked, rolling my hips against him, each touch amplified to a point where I didn't know if I could last much longer. I felt him drink deeply, felt myself flow into him, and I never in my wildest imagination would have imagined it could feel so amazing, so fulfilling, so... right.

"Damien, I don't think I can—"

"Don't," he said, pulling away just enough to stare into my eyes. "Don't hold back. Don't stop."

My chest heaved as I tried to draw in air, and I met his molten gaze, falling into the depths of his eyes in a way that promised no return.

I never wanted to return, never wanted to escape.

"Come undone for me," he said, his fingers digging into my hips as he guided me into the rhythm, lifting his hips to meet me. I gasped at the spot he hit, at the release beckoning me into the abyss. "I want to feel you shatter around my cock. Cry out my name for the world to hear."

He pulled me down with him, kissing me hungrily, and we fell into sync, consuming each other, losing ourselves to one another. I'd been long lost to him, time and time again, in this life and past lives, and I'd do it all over again. As long as I had him, I didn't care what we faced, what we encountered.

He cursed against my lips as his body tightened beneath me, and I cried out, pleasure rolling through me as he lifted his hips to thrust into me once more. His head dipped back to the pillow as he joined me in his own release.

My arms quivered as I held myself up, my curls spilling over my shoulders and around my face as I gazed down at him. He lifted his eyes to me, a breathless smile curving his lips as he lifted his hand to cup my cheeks.

"Gods, you're beautiful."

My cheeks flushed at his words, my heart fluttering in my chest.

"Happy Solstice," he breathed, eyes trailing over my face.

I smiled, placing my hand over his as I melted into his touch. "Happy Solstice."

His eyes rose to the window, and he let out a breath. "How late did I sleep?"

"Not too late," I said, leaning down to brush my nose against his before kissing him and rising from the bed.

"Is *Mitera* here already?" he asked as I ran to the bathroom to clean myself up.

"She is. She's down in the kitchen."

When I returned from the bathroom I found him sitting on the edge of the bed, rubbing his hand over his face.

"I have something for you," I said as I stepped into my underwear and pulled my sweater back over my head before heading for the door, not caring that I was only in an oversized sweater that barely covered my underwear. It was what I'd worn all morning, and it wasn't anything Ethel hadn't seen.

His brows rose as he pulled his pants on.

"I'll be right back. You stay here," I said, attempting to tuck my frazzled curls back into place behind my ears before giving up.

He huffed a laugh as I disappeared out our door and hurried down the stairs.

Ethel turned, gray eyebrows rising as I entered the kitchen. "Is he up?"

I nodded, and she quickly grabbed the basket sitting on the counter.

"Here ye go, love," she said, eyes lighting up. "Good luck."

"Thank you so much, *Mitera*," I said, taking the basket and turning to head back up to the room.

CHAPTER 19

DAMIEN

The door groaned as it opened, revealing Cassie carrying something, and my brows furrowed at the basket with a linen cloth folded over whatever the contents were.

Then, the scent hit me: the sweet, tart aroma I hadn't smelled in over nine hundred years, and my heart soared and plummeted all at once. My thoughts halted, and I couldn't bring myself to rise from the bed as she drew closer.

"What..." I said, choking on the words as she set the basket beside me and sat down.

"This isn't your true Solstice gift, but I thought it would be a perfect way to start the day," she said nervously as she nodded to the basket. "Go ahead."

My eyes fell back to the basket, and I reached out to pull away the cloth, revealing pastries overflowing with the rich red berry filling I knew all too well. Chaza berries. They were almost the same as the ones Mother used to make for us as children. I hadn't tasted one since she'd been killed all those centuries ago.

My vision blurred as the sorrow melted together with happiness welling in my chest. I lifted my eyes to her, blinking back tears. "How did you..."

"I remember you telling me about your favorite sweet on our first date," she said, fidgeting with the sleeve of her sweater. "I'd wanted to make it for you, but you told me the berries didn't grow around here."

I looked down at the pastries, steam rising from them, the scent of chaza berry flooding my lungs with each breath. It was my childhood, every bit of what I missed, every bit of what I never got to say goodbye to.

"The memory I had of us decorating the tree—you placed dried chaza berries as decorations, and it was then that I remembered." She smiled, but there was something somber about it, a sadness that touched her hazel eyes. "I still can't remember her face, or what her name was. I just know that she made these for us—for you—and how special it was. I asked Thalia if she could find a way to get chaza berries from the Godsrealm. They weren't too difficult to work with, and I hope I did the pastries justice. I couldn't quite remember how they looked."

"They're perfect," I whispered as I smiled at her, loving how flustered she got. "*You're* perfect."

She blinked, and her fear melted into happiness as her lips curved into a smile. She nodded to the basket. "Try one before you go praising me."

I reached out and took one, the crust crumbling beneath my touch. They were warm. "Did you make these this morning?"

She nodded eagerly. "I've been up since six making them. I wanted to surprise you."

Gods, did she even sleep? I'd gotten in around four, and she'd been pacing the hallway when I arrived.

I took a bite, and my eyes slid shut as the sweet and tart filling met my tongue. Gods, it was just as I remembered, the crust buttery and flakey with just the right amount of crunch before it gave way to the soft, chewy center. She'd told me she loved to bake, and I wondered if a part of her remembered how to make them, because there was nothing that compared. It was the same.

"Damien?" she said, a look of worry painting her face, and I realized tears were rolling down my cheeks.

"Sorry," I said, brushing them away. "I... I haven't had one of these since the last time she made them for me. I would've been... eleven? Twelve, maybe?"

The inner corners of her brows curved upward.

"Try one; they're perfect. They taste just like how she used to make them," I said, nodding to the basket.

She blinked and looked down to the basket. "Really? You like it?"

"I love it," I corrected, smiling as she took one of the pastries and bit into it.

She moaned at the taste. "Oh my god, these are delicious!"

I huffed a laugh.

"They're almost like a cherry, but... Wait, no, it's sweeter, like a... blueberry? No, that's not right." The way her brows scrunched together left me unable to fight the laughter.

"Thank you," I said before taking another bite.

She smiled. "Well, that's not your only gift."

I cocked an eyebrow at her. "Does that mean I get to unwrap you again tonight?"

She elbowed me and I huffed a laugh. "You'll have to wait and see."

CHAPTER 20

CASSIE

"Please behave yourself," I begged Barrett as I headed for the door.

"You say that as if I cause trouble," Barrett said before a smug grin crept across his face.

"You say that as if you don't." I opened the door to greet Mom and Dad.

"Hey, sweetheart!" Mom said, her hazel eyes lighting up. God, I'd missed those eyes, missed seeing them every day. She threw her arms out and wrapped me in a tight hug.

I squeezed her just as tightly. "Hey, Mom."

Mom released me just in time for Dad to pull me into a big hug, lifting me up until my feet were dangling and laughter burst from my lips.

"It's been too long," he said into my ear.

I pulled back and arched a brow at him. "You say that like it's been months."

"It feels like it," he said before setting me back on my feet.

Mom glanced at Barrett as she started removing her gloves. "Hey, Barrett."

"Hey, Mrs. Hites. Mr. Hites," he said, giving a light nod of his head.

"Behaving yourself I hope," Mom teased.

"You know I'm not," he said, donning a smug grin.

She huffed a laugh and turned to me. "Where's Damien?"

"He's in the kitchen, helping *Mitera* set things up for dinner."

Her smile widened into a grin. "Oh, *Mitera's* here? I was hoping I'd get to see her again. She was so sweet. I'm glad we were able to meet her on your birthday."

"She's amazing."

"I'll take your coat for you," Barrett offered, and Mom's brows rose.

"Why thank you, Barrett," she said, turning her back to him as he helped her out of her jacket.

I narrowed my eyes at him suspiciously, to which he gave me an incredulous look. "What? I can be a gentleman."

When you want something.

"Merry Christmas!" Kat called out from down the hall.

"Kat!" Mom exclaimed, hurrying to hug her. "Merry Christmas, hun."

"Barrett, could ye go gather some firewood fer me?" Ethel called out.

"On it!" Barrett called out as he slid past Mom and Kat to head for the kitchen.

I caught sight of Dad eyeing the hallway skeptically. It wasn't as if it was the first time he'd been here, but dread curled in my stomach at the look in his eyes.

"Come on; everyone's in the kitchen," I said, starting down the hallway. "*Mitera's* made some snacks for us to enjoy. Would you guys like a drink?"

"Something warm if you have it, please," Mom said, rubbing her hands together.

They followed me into the kitchen where Ethel was still working to prepare dinner, the scent of roasted turkey and spiced apples filled the room. The aroma dragged a hum of excitement from Dad, and it was a relief to see him warm up to something.

"Oh it smells wonderful in here," Mom said.

Damien lifted his gaze, and he smiled as we neared the island. "Hot cider anyone?"

"Oh that would be lovely," she said as she stepped toward Damien and gave him a hug. "I hope you've been well."

"Busy but can't complain." He ladled some of the steaming drink into a glass for her, dropped a stick of cinnamon and slivers of fruit on the top, and slid it over to her. She thanked him before taking a sip, and I stopped at his side, pressing a kiss to his cheek as he handed me mine.

"Wow, this is so good," Mom said, and Dad came to a stop at her side before she offered it for him to try.

"Been workin' on it all mornin'," Ethel said, glancing back from where she, Anna, and Thalia were peeling potatoes.

"Would you like one, Mr. Hites?" Damien offered.

He looked at him for a moment, and I feared he might turn him down, but he nodded. "Sure."

Damien began preparing his drink, and I snuck over to Ethel to peer over her shoulder, finding a blend of purples, oranges, reds, and whites laid out on the sheet pan of vegetables. "Are those the carrots we harvested from Anna's garden?"

Anna smiled warmly. "They are."

"They're gonnae taste delicious," Ethel said as she finished peeling her potato.

I pressed a kiss to Ethel's cheek, and she chuckled. "Everything you make is delicious."

"Comin' through!" Barrett called as he backed into the door, arms loaded down with logs.

"Need help?" Dad asked, and I blinked before sliding a nervous glance at Damien, who looked equally nervous.

"Sure," Barrett said, and Dad followed him into the living room.

I hurried over to Mom's side, leaning in to whisper, "Is Dad okay?"

She let out a breath, setting her glass on the countertop. "He's been a bit moody the past couple of days. Stress at work has him on edge, and he's been worried about you."

"I'm doing fine," I said. "Honestly, I'm doing a lot better than I was a few weeks ago."

She turned her gaze to me, and for a moment she seemed to look over my face before lifting her hand to my cheek. "Are you sleeping better?"

"It's getting better," I said. "I started seeing a therapist."

Her brows rose. "Really?"

I nodded. "She's amazing, and patient. We're taking it slow, but I think it's gonna help."

"Dad will warm up. Just give him some time," she said, her voice full of the love that had gotten me through so many dark times in my life. "Show him he's wrong to worry. Let him see you and them together. Let him see your happiness as I do."

Warmth filled my chest, and it was a relief that she saw what I did.

I glanced at Ethel. "Is there any way I can help?"

"Nah, love. Zephyr and Vincent are chopping firewood out back, and Ah've got all the help Ah need here," she said, glancing over her shoulder. "Ye relax."

"I'd fuckin' love to hear you say that again!" Barrett's voice cut across the chatter in the kitchen. I stiffened, my eyes flying to the hallway, and before I could think to act, Damien was rushing through the doorway.

"Stay here," I pleaded to the others before Mom and I hurried after him.

"You don't know half the shit he's done for her," Barrett growled as Damien stepped between them. "Where were you when they took her? I didn't see you searching the woods with us. No you relied on the police to find her."

"Guys, this is not the time or place," Damien said, glancing between them, arms outstretched.

"She's changed since *he* came into the picture," Dad said, gesturing to Damien. "She doesn't talk to us anymore, rarely visits—"

"Did you ever think that maybe she needed to get out? That you were suffocating her?" Barrett pressed against Damien's hand, his eyes locked on Dad in a way that promised violence. "What about how her apartment looked after she was taken?"

Damien shot Barrett a look of warning. "Barrett."

"No! This is bullshit." Barrett's steel eyes were full of a kind of anger that left me speechless. "You wanna be here? You'll respect her fuckin' decision. Don't forget the reason she's here is because of *him*," he shouted, nodding to Damien. "Because *he* didn't give up!"

"Barrett!" Damien yelled, and Barrett's gaze snapped to him.

Dad's hands were balled into fists at his side. "You think I liked waiting at home for her to possibly never come back? I didn't know where to even begin to look for her. Her whole life all I wanted to do was keep her safe, get her to her next birthday. Now I'm powerless to do that."

I stiffened, and my eyes flitted to Damien, fearful he might have caught onto the near slip up.

Dad continued. "She's been so secretive since she started hanging out with you guys, and then after her birthday, she just cuts off communication with us for days. What am I supposed to think of that?"

I stormed forward. "You can think that I'm a grown woman and I'm going through things."

His eyes shot to me, as if he hadn't even realized I'd been standing there through everything he said.

"I hit a low spot. I've had my bad days. But it's because of them— because of Damien—that I'm here right now. He's been there for me every waking moment. He's comforted me when the nightmares keep me from sleep, pushing me to be healthier, to exercise and get out of the house, to go to therapy. He's pushing me to better myself, and I'm thankful every day I have him," I said, my voice breaking at the admission of just how bad I'd been, how low I'd gotten.

"Apologize," I said, my hands tightening into fits. "Now. Or you can leave."

He swallowed, and Mom remained in the doorway, silent, her fear sending waves of frost over my skin.

"I—" Dad's eyes flitted to Damien before they returned to me. "I just want to make sure you're safe, that you're okay."

"I am," I said, my words clipped. "Now apologize."

He let out a ragged sigh. "Sorry. I shouldn't have said anything."

Damien nodded his head before glancing to Barrett, whose gaze remained fixed on Dad.

"It's the holidays," Damien said, and I didn't miss the brief glance he slid my way, the concern in his eyes. "We're supposed to be celebrating."

Vincent appeared in the doorway. "Anna called me from the log pile. Is everything okay?"

"It is now," Damien said, nudging Barrett toward him. "Get Barrett a drink."

I followed after Damien, glancing back at Dad as Mom walked over to him. The look of disappointment and near anger on her face as she stopped in front of him surprised me. I turned, leaving them to speak as we returned to the kitchen.

"That was awkward," Kat whispered as she slid into the chair next to mine.

I let out a sigh. "I had a feeling something was gonna happen with Dad. I'm just glad it didn't result in Barrett kicking his ass."

"Yay family drama," Kat deadpanned before she reached into her pocket. "I have something for you."

My brows rose, and I shot up. "Wait, I have something for you, too!"

I hurried down the hall and into the living room, thankful Mom and Dad had stepped out to talk as I grabbed Kat's gift from the table of presents everyone had stashed for the exchange later that night.

"Here," I said as I returned, holding out the small box, and her fern green eyes lit up as she took it before handing me mine.

We opened them at the same time, the way we always did, always too excited to see what the other thought to be able to choose who went first. As I tore the wrapping away and lifted the lid, my eyes trailed over the golden locket laid out atop black velvet, over the delicate pattern of a crescent moon and constellations engraved in metal.

"Aw, Kat," I said, hooking my finger under the delicate chain and lifting it to look at it closer.

"Cas!" Kat cried out as she finished unearthing her gift from the wrapping paper, lifting her own locket into the air.

We looked at each other and belted out into laughter—we'd gotten each other nearly the same thing.

"There's a picture in there already," Kat said, eyes lighting up as she leaned in. "Open it!"

I snickered, and opened the locket to find not one, but two pictures, and for a moment, my eyes started to burn, tears welling in my eyes. On one side was a picture of her and me from our first day of first grade together. We looked so different at six, her coppery hair tied into twin braids, while mine was pulled half back so it was out of my face. I remembered it as if it were yesterday: how I'd cried, too afraid to leave Mom's side no matter how much she encouraged me. Kat had comforted me, held my hand and managed to convince me to leave the safety of the car.

My eyes drifted to the other picture, and I couldn't stop the smile from spreading across my face if I wanted to. It was a picture from one of our pizza dates at Gallina's. Kat had me tucked under her arm, her head resting sideways atop mine as she stuck her tongue out and threw up a peace sign. My eyes were closed, my lips open as I laughed, my nose dotted with pizza sauce she'd gotten on me before looping me in for a surprise picture. My laughter echoed in the memory as it resurfaced.

"I love it," I said, glancing to the side to see her looking at the picture I'd placed in her locket. A faint smile tugged at the corners of her lips, her eyes latched onto the portrait of us on Halloween—her in her witchy attire, and me flashing my fangs.

"I love you," she said, wrapping her arms around me, and I hugged her tightly. I caught sight of Damien from where he stood nearby, chatting with Zephyr and Anna as he slid me a glance, his eyes full of the same love I felt for him.

I released Kat in time to see Mom and Dad step back into the kitchen, and my heart launched into my throat, but the look of remorse on Dad's face forced me to glance at Mom, who gave me an apologetic smile.

Dad leaned in and pressed a kiss to my forehead. "I'm sorry, baby girl. I shouldn't have acted that way."

I offered him a smile. "Thank you."

"I'm gonna go talk to Damien, if that's okay with you," he said.

I swallowed and glanced nervously at Damien. "Um."

"I promise I'll behave," he assured me, and I nodded.

He offered me a smile and walked toward Damien whose brows rose when he caught sight of him. They exchanged words briefly before continuing to the back door, and Damien shared a smile of reassurance with me before following him onto the back porch.

"They'll be okay," Mom said, settling into a chair next to me.

"Promise?" I asked, glancing at her.

She smiled at me, and I couldn't help but feel comfort from it. "I promise."

CHAPTER 21

DAMIEN

"Well I guess that wasn't a total disaster," I said, shooting a look at Barrett.

Barrett didn't seem to hear me. That, or he just chose to outright ignore me through his conversation with Vincent, a glass of cider in his hand. I had a feeling he'd spiked the drink with something stronger than the rum Cassie's Dad had added to his after our talk.

Cassie let out a slow breath. "Yeah. I hope your talk with Dad wasn't too awkward."

I huffed a laugh. "It was awkward enough."

The door closed behind me, and I turned to find Cassie's father awkwardly kicking gravel at the foot of the stairway.

"I owe you a better apology," he said, and I shoved my hands into my coat pockets. I didn't know what he had said, but the way Barrett had acted, I knew it hadn't been a simple remark. It didn't matter, though. The last thing Cassie needed was for me and her father to be fighting.

He drew a deep breath and ran his hand over the back of his neck. "When Barrett started talking about you and Cassie, I—"

"I don't care what you said to him," I said as I reached the foot of the stairs, and his eyes lifted to me. He blinked, opening and closing his mouth for a moment, seeming shocked at my words. "It's not important."

The way he had looked at me, at Barrett... I didn't blame him for how he felt—could only imagine what he was thinking and feeling. He and her mother were in the dark, oblivious to the truth. Still, it didn't change the way he'd spoken to my brother, who had done nothing but sacrifice for Cassie time and time again.

We stood in awkward silence, and I contemplated leaving him out here alone, but that only further the divide between Cassie and her family. She didn't need that.

"I should've never gone off like that," he said, shifting on his feet. "Barrett's a good guy. I see how happy she is here, and how well you guys treat her. It irritated me at first, seeing her so happy without us, but I shouldn't have reacted that way. It was wrong of me."

The trees danced in the winter wind, and I remained silent, watching him, listening to what more he might say.

"Thank you," he finally said, and I blinked. "I know you don't understand where I'm coming from as a father, but..."

Agony tore through me, winding and twisting deep in my chest, but I didn't let it show. I understood how he felt more than he would ever know—to watch your child suffer and be helpless to do anything about it...

His eyes lifted to me. "Thank you so much for being there for her when I couldn't."

"I will always be there for her," I said, meeting his gaze as relief shined in his eyes. "I promise."

Barrett slapped his hand on his thigh, catching everyone's attention. "All right, now that the humans are gone." Barrett's eyes shifted to Cassie. "No offense, Cas."

She narrowed her eyes, but her lips curved into a grin as she curled closer to me, and I pulled her in, relishing in the feel of her body against mine.

"I'll let it slide," she said.

"It's time for the gift exchange." Barrett set his drink on the coffee table. "I think since it's her first Solstice, Cas should get us started."

Cassie stiffened in my arms, her eyes widening. "Me?"

"Who'd you get?" he asked, crossing his arms.

She chewed her lip as she stood and headed for the presents, grabbing a small blue box with a bow. "You," she muttered as she held out the box to him. "It's nothing special."

Barrett blinked, clearly taken back by her admission, and his eyes fell to the box. "You got *me*?"

She nodded. "Take it before I decide to give you coal instead."

He cocked a brow. "Coal?"

"You know, coal?"

I huffed a laugh when Barrett continued to frown at her, clearly not aware of the Christmas traditions some mortals shared.

Cassie continued, her words a flurry as her cheeks turned pink when her joke fell on deaf ears. "It's—it's... Just open it," she grumbled, shoving the small box into his hands before hurrying back to me.

"I'm sure he'll love it," I whispered into her ear as she slouched on the couch.

"He better. I searched forever for something," she said, watching as he opened the box.

Barrett removed the lid of the small box, and for a moment, he stared at what was inside.

"Well?" Cassie said, shifting in her seat.

I lifted my chin, trying to catch a glimpse of what she'd gotten him.

He lifted up a single black pendant earring. Dangling from the small hoop was a black dagger, not quite like the weapons we wielded but similar still.

"I didn't really know what you liked, but I know your ear's pierced, so I thought you might like a new earring," she said nervously, as if she needed to explain the gift.

He smiled as he looked at it and, without saying a word, he set the box down, before reaching up to replace the earring he wore with the one Cassie had gifted him. He dropped his hands and turned his head to the side. "How do I look?"

"Sexeh!" James chanted.

"I think it looks great on you," Cassie said with a warm smile, her happiness filling my lungs like the scent of wildflowers. I wished she could always feel this happy. I'd have drowned in it if I could.

"Thanks, Cas," he said, hurrying over to her and pressing a kiss to her cheek. "I love it."

She smiled warmly. "You're welcome."

"I think Zephyr should go next," Vincent said, and Zephyr drew a deep breath before heading to grab another present.

Zephyr gifted Anna a basket of what he swore were top of the line garden tools, and I'd never seen her smile so widely. After that, one by one everyone exchanged gifts. Thalia had gifted Vincent a baby carrier, and Cassie had nearly melted at the thought of Vincent carrying around what he swore was a baby girl. Vincent gifted James a new pair of earbuds to block out Barrett and Thalia's arguments while he worked, to which I'd barked out a laugh. Barrett had proudly gifted Thalia a set of lingerie, to which I'd rolled my eyes.

"You wish you could see me in this," she teased, inspecting the delicate maroon lace.

"Maybe one day I will," he taunted, and she narrowed her eyes at him before laying the fabric back in its box.

"Thalia's just too in love to find the words for how she feels," Barrett said before she could say another word, and her lips parted as he looked at me. "You're last, Damien."

Cassie snickered as Thalia started to argue with Barrett, who waved his hand at her.

"I know, I know it's just the perfect gift and you can't wait to wear it," Barrett said, turning his back to her. "It's okay, Thalia. I understand how touched you are, but Gods, it's not like you to be so lost for words. I'm touched you love it so much."

I slid my arm out from under Cassie and rose from the couch as Barrett and Thalia proceeded to bait each other before it quickly escalated to them bickering. Cassie watched me with curious eyes as I grabbed the box I'd wrapped just a few days ago.

"Here," I said, holding it out to her, and Barrett and Thalia quieted, curiosity outweighing their argument.

She took it eagerly, excitement painted across her sweet face as she set the box in her lap. The others tilted their heads as she tore into the wrapping. I hoped she liked it.

Her eyes lit up as she opened the box to find a few items inside.

"I wasn't quite sure what to get you, so I got you a few things," I admitted as I eased onto the couch beside her.

She began pulling out the contents. First was a paper bag with Elythian inscriptions written across the paper. She frowned as she tried and failed to read them before glancing at me.

"It's Sonnun tea," I explained. "It's an herb from the Godsrealm that can grant dreamless sleep. It's hard to come by, but it helped you once before, so I thought it would be worth the effort."

Lucia had suffered terrible nightmares for a long while after I found her, and this had been one of the few things that had aided her until she could work through the ghosts haunting her.

She unfolded the top and smelled the tea before letting out a near groan of satisfaction, looking up at me with wide eyes. "Oh my god. It smells amazing."

A smile tugged at my lips as she set the bag aside and reached in for the next item with an excitement I hadn't seen since she'd walked into her library for the first time.

The next item was a book, and she turned it over to see the title. Sadly, she wouldn't be able to read it; I would have to help her.

"It's a book of legends from The Godsrealm," I explained. "I can read it to you if you like."

"Oh my goodness, I'd love that," she said excitedly before flipping through the book to find the illustrations decorating the pages. She stopped on the drawing of the Eternis Moth, its wings inked out across the full spread of the pages.

"I'd love for you to read these stories to me," she said, and for a moment her smile turned somber. "I want to learn everything I can."

I pressed a kiss to her forehead. "Anytime you want I'll read it to you. Maybe I can teach you the language."

Her gaze snapped to me, her hazel eyes lighting up. "Would you?"

"Of course. We all can help in that," I said, nodding to the others, who all murmured their agreements.

She set the book aside and looked into the box. She frowned as she caught sight of the last item, and as she pulled out the little package, she lifted her eyes to me. "White charcoal?"

I fought the smug grin on my face. "It's for your art."

She looked back down at the package. "Wait, I think I've heard of it."

I scooted closer to her, tilting my head to look at the white sticks in her hand. "You use a lot of charcoal. I found this when I stopped into an art supply shop, and I thought it would be perfect." I slid a smug grin her way. "So you might add some light to your darkness."

She turned her face to me, and I could see her fighting a smile. She drew her lower lip between her teeth, and she let out a snicker as she looked back down at her gift.

"Gods, what a sap," Barrett said, huffing a laugh.

"Perhaps you should take some lessons from him," Thalia said, knocking back her drink. "Maybe you could finally woo one of those females you're always talking to."

"Don't need romance when you've got these looks," he said, wiggling his eyebrows at her, to which she rolled her eyes.

Cassie shifted closer to me, drawing my attention back to her as she pressed a kiss to my lips. "They're perfect."

CHAPTER 22
CASSIE

The front door closed, and I looked over my shoulder as Damien reappeared in the living room after seeing everyone off. "Well, that was fun."

I snickered. "Maybe we should have let them stay the night. Sounds like you miss them already."

"I love them, but I want you to myself," he said as he eased onto the couch.

I stood, and his brows furrowed. "You leaving me, too?"

"I'll be right back," I said, and I kissed his cheek before hurrying to my library where his second gift was tucked away. Excitement swelled in my chest as I found the present, wrapped in the prettiest metallic black paper, and returned to his side. I stopped at the edge of the couch when I realized he also had a present in his lap, a coy smile on his face.

"Looks like I wasn't the only one who couldn't settle on one thing," he said.

A sheepish smile spread across my face. "It's nothing special. I thought you might like it, though."

I held out the present for him as I sat down on the couch, and he pulled at the paper, revealing a book. His eyes trailed over the cover.

"It's the first book in a series I think you'd love. I hoped maybe you might be able to read more... like you used to." One corner of his lips kicked up, and I continued. "Sabriel is one of my favorites. It's a story about a girl whose necromancer father goes missing."

"Sounds like you might need to make room for me in that library," he teased.

A snicker bubbled up my throat and I nudged him with my shoulder. "I think I can spare a bookshelf.

"Maybe I'll start it tonight," he said, absentmindedly flipping through the pages.

My eyes lit up. "Really?"

He nodded before holding the wrapped present out to me. "Your turn."

I took the box, my smile widening as I lifted the lid. My hands stilled as I found a dagger nestled inside, a mirror image of the one he'd given me a month ago, but...

My brows furrowed, and I lifted my gaze to him.

"A twin to your dagger," he said, as if in explanation. "The way you pulled my dagger and used it and yours, against me, I thought you might be well suited for dual wielding."

"You really think I could?" I asked.

"Won't know until you try," he said with a shrug. "You can start practicing, feel it out."

Something swelled in my chest, a combination of excitement, pride, and adoration building until I wasn't sure I could contain it. I set the present aside to wrap my arms around his neck.

"Thank you," I breathed, tears dotting my lashes.

"For what?" he asked, his arms coming around me.

"For everything," I said, unable to stop the tears from rolling down my cheek. "I felt so lost after everything happened. I know it's not over, that it's gonna take time to work through it all, but I'm getting there. Thank you for reaching out, for helping me find my way out."

He squeezed me tighter. "I will always find you, no matter how tightly the darkness holds you. I will always be there to pull you out."

To be continued...

EPILOGUE
SELENE

Something was wrong.

Something was...corrupted.

Something that should have never been touched by anyone had somehow been defiled in a way that would make Celestia herself weep.

The acrid, tainted feeling had clawed its way deep into my bones, lingering far longer than it should, and I feared it was beginning to manifest into something I would be powerless to stop. Powerless to face.

I pushed myself from my bed, sleep evading me once more. How many days had it been since I had last found rest? Ten? Twenty? There was no true way to judge the passage of time here, no rise or fall of a sun to mark the beginning and end. It changed nothing, though. There was no beginning anymore, not for me. Only an end. And I wondered how much longer it would be before what I had done finally caught up with me.

The room spun as I stood, and tiny clawed hands grabbed hold of mine to steady me. My eyes fell to the astral sprites gathering around my legs, their bodies made of pure night sky—galaxies, stars and constellations dancing in the dark, misty depths, their glowing eyes like distant suns staring up at me in quiet concern.

I lifted my gaze to the gold framed mirror leaning against the wall, finding the ghostly reflection of what I once was. My hair dragged along the marble in silver waves as I stepped closer to the glass, the strands laying over my shoulders and back like a cloak, barely revealing the pale undergarments I wore. The astral sprites hurried around my legs, brushing through the silver locks, climbing onto one another to reach higher places as they worked their way through the tangles. Their chitters sent warmth through my chest, one of the only things to give me a sense of joy in this place.

A presence brushed over my skin, one I'd avoided a little over a week ago, and I turned. My magic resisted as I attempted to summon my gown, and I let out a heavy sigh of exhaustion as I failed to manifest it. An astral sprite tapped at my leg, and I looked down to find it and several others offering a silver slip.

"Thank you," I whispered with a soft smile before stepping into the gown and pulling the straps over my shoulders. It would have to do.

On weak legs, I started for the door, and the sprites hurried before me, opening it to let me onto the dais where Damien stood, looking for me. I straightened my posture, shoving back the exhaustion as I stepped toward the stairs, my hands folded neatly in front of me.

He knelt at the foot of the steps. "Goddess."

"You may rise, warrior," I said, my gaze sweeping over him. He looked healthier than the last time I had seen him, the color returning to his olive skin, and I couldn't stifle the hint of relief.

"Apologies for not coming to you sooner," he said as he rose. "I've been busy. I tried to see you a little over a week ago, but—"

"I was attending to something of importance," I said, the lie slipping from my tongue all too easily, the words joining the other lies as they festered deep within me like poison.

"I figured I might give you an update on—"

"It is Solstice," I said, noting the scent of jasmine and citrus on his skin, the hint of... My brows furrowed. Chaza berries? I ignored it. "I will not ask you to work tonight. It can wait until tomorrow."

He blinked, as if surprised I was willing to give him a day off, that I was allowing him to disregard his duties for the sake of a holiday. I deserved that look, deserved everything he threw at me with each moment of his avoidance, spite, resentment. I'd done this to myself, made myself out to be the cold cruel creature he knew me as, despite what it cost me.

"You may return to your celebration. I won't keep you from your mate," I said, turning to return to my room. To my oblivion.

"Wait."

LUNA LAURIER

I stiffened and turned to look back at him over my shoulder, his foot planted on the bottom step, as if he were about to follow me.

"I... uh," His eyes left mine briefly, and he shifted on his feet. "I thought I'd bring you something. A gift."

My brows furrowed as I turned to him fully, and he made his way up the steps, a bundle of linen fabric in his hands. A gift?

"I know how much you enjoyed them when my mother made them," he said, and my heart plummeted as the scent of chaza berries grew stronger—rich and decadent. He pulled back the cloth to reveal the small pastry, rich burgundy filling nestled within a flaky crust.

My lips parted, but I didn't know what to say. I hadn't seen the fruit, let alone tasted it in centuries.

"Happy Solstice," he said, albeit reluctantly. His lips didn't curve into a smile. His eyes didn't light up as they used to when he was young, but deep within his warm silver eyes there was a hint of something. Hope? Hope that the goddess who had once been so close to him might still linger somewhere deep within me.

I hesitated but took the pastry. "Thank you."

He took a step back, his hands awkwardly falling to his side.

"You made this?" I asked.

"Cas did." His eyes briefly flickered to mine before slipping away.

Cas. It felt strange to hear the name. No matter what face she took, no matter what name she returned to me with, she would always be Moira. A child of fate. *My* child of fate.

"Thank you," I said once more, and he nodded before turning to walk away. My gaze followed him to the entrance, shadows at his feet as he left, returning to his mate. His family.

His happiness.

"I'm so sorry for what I've put you through..." I whispered as he vanished, and something twisted in my chest. My knees quivered, and the crushing loneliness of my temple returned in his wake as I fell to the marble floor.

"I hope you can forgive me for what you will likely face," I said, able to speak freely in his absence. "Fates watch over you for what you will have to suffer for my mistakes. All for giving into my selfish desires."

My vision blurred as I lowered my eyes to the pastry, and the memories danced through my thoughts like falling stars, the face of one of my dearest friends—her smile and laugher cascading across my mind before dying out. The memories were both my haven and my hell.

"I hope you can forgive me for what I subjected your son to, Carissa. For what my selfish actions cost you in the end," I whispered, something building in the back of my throat. "I hope you and Marius found peace in Elysium, that you watch over them."

121

The empty space pressed in on the walls of my mind, and sobs broke from my throat, milky tears rolling down my cheeks before dripping onto the silk of my gown.

"I'm so sorry for everything."

Luna Laurier's Taste of Darkness

Can't get enough of the Shadow and Moonlight Universe and it's characters? Join the Patreon to gain access to bonus scenes and content not in the books, bonus spicy scenes between characters (both canon and non-canon *eyes the spicy scene between Cassie, Damien, and Marcus*), NSFW artwork, ARC Team access, discounts on merch and signed books, and more!

---

www.patreon.com/lunalaurier

SHOP THE OFFICIAL MERCH STORE

LUNALAURIER.COM

ACKNOWLEDGEMENT

This little winter novella has become more than I ever imagined in to be. A story of finding your way out of the depths of depression and finding joy in the seasons.

To my husband, my love, you are my rock, and I couldn't imagine riding this rollercoaster of a journey without you at my side.

To my son, you drive me forward when the voices tell me to quit.

To Vhexi and Fey, thank you for helping me orchestrate all the heartbreak

To my amazing developmental editor, Natalie Cammaratta. Here's to all the future side eyes and trauma I will put you through.

To my amazing copy editor/proofreader, Alexa with The Fiction Fix. Thank you for teaching me all you have.

To my amazing artist, Huangja, who has breathed life into my charactesr and brought them to life on the pages.

To my fellow authors: Kristen M. Long, K.A. Lee, Amber Nicole, Kalista Neith, Nicole Kimmons, Jamie Applegate-Hunter, Nik Robbins, Jeneane Oreilly, Allie Shante, J.D. Linton, Allison Aldridge, Sydne Barnett, and Jordan A. Day, thank you for always being there for me when I need it most. I have never felt more seen or validated than I do when I speak to you. I am so blessed to be able to call you besties!

To my kickass Beta Team. Nicole, Kat, Brittany, Ava, Rikki, and Amber, you have helped transform this story in more ways than you could imagine. You have directly influenced this story, and will forever hold a special place in my heart.

To my amazing ARC Team, I could never thank you enough. You are always there for me, lifting this series up, and encouraging me to continue forward.

To my amazing friends, followers, and supporters on TikTok, Instagram, and Facebook. You're kind words, your encouragement, your excitement push me forward, and it has been a light in my life when I was ready to give up.

And lastly, to my readers. Thank you for taking a chance on me. I could not have done this without you. Thank you for all your support. I am forever grateful.

Printed in the USA
CPSIA information can be obtained
at www.ICGtesting.com
JSHW082027271223
54278JS00005B/24